Precious Time

The Chronicles of Kerrigan Sequel, Volume 6

W.J. May

Published by Dark Shadow Publishing, 2017.

This is a work of fiction. Similarities to real people, places, or events are entirely coincidental.

PRECIOUS TIME

First edition. May 10, 2017.

Copyright © 2017 W.J. May.

Written by W.J. May.

Also by W.J. May

Bit-Lit Series
Lost Vampire
Cost of Blood
Price of Death

Blood Red Series
Courage Runs Red
The Night Watch
Marked by Courage
Forever Night

Daughters of Darkness: Victoria's Journey
Victoria
Huntress
Coveted (A Vampire & Paranormal Romance)
Twisted

Hidden Secrets Saga
Seventh Mark - Part 1
Seventh Mark - Part 2
Marked By Destiny
Compelled
Fate's Intervention
Chosen Three
The Hidden Secrets Saga: The Complete Series

Prophecy Series
Only the Beginning

The Chronicles of Kerrigan

Rae of Hope
Dark Nebula
House of Cards
Royal Tea
Under Fire
End in Sight
Hidden Darkness
Twisted Together
Mark of Fate
Strength & Power
Last One Standing
Rae of Light
The Chronicles of Kerrigan Box Set Books # 1 - 6

The Chronicles of Kerrigan: Gabriel
Living in the Past

The Chronicles of Kerrigan Prequel
Christmas Before the Magic
Question the Darkness
Into the Darkness
Fight the Darkness
Alone in the Darkness
Lost in Darkness
The Chronicles of Kerrigan Prequel Series Books #1-3

The Chronicles of Kerrigan Sequel
A Matter of Time
Time Piece
Second Chance
Glitch in Time
Our Time
Precious Time

The Hidden Secrets Saga
Seventh Mark (part 1 & 2)

The Senseless Series
Radium Halos
Radium Halos - Part 2
Nonsense

Standalone
Shadow of Doubt (Part 1 & 2)
Five Shades of Fantasy
Shadow of Doubt - Part 2
Four and a Half Shades of Fantasy
Full Moon
Dream Fighter
What Creeps in the Night
Forest of the Forbidden
HuNted
Arcane Forest: A Fantasy Anthology
Ancient Blood of the Vampire and Werewolf

The Chronicles of Kerrigan Sequel
Precious Time
Book 6
By W.J. May
Copyright 2017 by W.J. May

This e-book is licensed for your personal enjoyment only. This e-book may not be re-sold or given away to other people. If you would like to share this book with another person, please purchase an additional copy for each recipient. If you're reading this book and did not purchase it, or it was not purchased for your use only, then please return to Smashwords.com and purchase your own copy. Thank you for respecting the hard work of the author.

All rights reserved. No part of this publication may be reproduced, stored in or introduced into a retrieval system, or transmitted, in any form, or by any means (electronic, mechanical, photocopying, recording, or otherwise) without the prior written permission of both the copyright owner and the above publisher of this book.

This is a work of fiction. Names, characters, places, brands, media, and incidents are either the product of the author's imagination or are used fictitiously. Any resemblance to actual person, living or dead, events, or locales is entirely coincidental. The author acknowledges the trademarked status and trademark owners of various products referenced in this work of fiction, which have been used without permission. The publication/use of these trademarks is not authorized, associated with, or sponsored by the trademark owners.

All rights reserved.
Copyright 2017 by W.J. May
Cover design by: Book Cover by Design

No part of this book may be used or reproduced in any manner whatsoever without written permission, except in the case of brief quotations embodied in articles and reviews.

Have You Read the C.o.K Prequel Series?

A Sub-Series of the Chronicles of Kerrigan.
A prequel on how Simon Kerrigan met Beth!!

PREQUEL –
   Christmas Before the Magic
   Question the Darkness
   Into the Darkness
   Fight the Darkness
   Alone the Darkness
   Lost the Darkness

The Chronicles of Kerrigan

Book I - *Rae of Hope* is FREE!
  Book Trailer:
  http://www.youtube.com/watch?v=gILAwXxx8MU
Book II - *Dark Nebula*
Book Trailer:
http://www.youtube.com/watch?v=Ca24STi_bFM
Book III - *House of Cards*
Book IV - *Royal Tea*
Book V - *Under Fire*
Book VI - *End in Sight*
Book VII – *Hidden Darkness*
Book VIII – *Twisted Together*
Book IX – *Mark of Fate*
Book X – *Strength & Power*
Book XI – *Last One Standing*
Book XII – *Rae of Light*

The Chronicles of Kerrigan SEQUEL

Matter of Time
    Time Piece
    Second Chance
    Glitch in Time
    Our Time
    Precious Time

PRECIOUS TIME

Don't want the Chronicles of Kerrigan to be over yet?

The Chronicles of Kerrigan: Gabriel

**COMING JULY 15th
PREORDER YOUR COPY TODAY!**

Find W.J. May

Website:
http://www.wanitamay.yolasite.com
Facebook:
https://www.facebook.com/pages/Author-WJ-May-FAN-PAGE/141170442608149
Newsletter:
SIGN UP FOR W.J. May's Newsletter to find out about new releases, updates, cover reveals and even freebies!
http://eepurl.com/97aYf

PRECIOUS TIME - Blurb:

How much can you hide before only the truth is left?

The stage is set, the players are ready, and the battle is about to begin...

After years of fighting, Rae Kerrigan and her friends find themselves at the end of the line. Only one remaining person stands in the way of them getting everything they'd ever wanted: Peace, safety, the chance for a normal life. But in Rae's case, that 'normal life' might include a little more than she bargained for.

Upon discovering she's pregnant, Rae finds herself in the most dangerous game of cat and mouse yet. The stakes have never been higher, the risks have never been greater, and when the gang squares off against Samantha Neilson once and for all—some difficult choices will have to be made.

What will it mean to have a baby who's not only a hybrid, but has three separate sets of ink? Should she tell Devon, knowing that the two of them are about to go into battle, and risk losing it all? Can she keep it a secret but marry him at the same time?

And as the day of judgement approaches...who can she really trust?

Chapter 1

'Time is measured not by clocks, but by moments.'

"...and then I was just standing there, wondering what was going on. Wondering about this weird feeling that had come over me. At first I thought it was just the trauma of the royal wedding, but we've all been through trauma before. That wasn't it. So then, I did something strange..."

Rae paused in her pacing long enough to pull in a gulping breath.

"I let all my abilities fall away. Released my hold on Jennifer's ink and every other set. They didn't disappear. I just made them go dormant for a moment." She sucked in a slow breath, trying to let her heart stop racing. "I just let my body decide what to do. Let it decide which tatù I needed. Made it a kind of...automatic response." It was hard to put into words what she'd done. Since realizing she had more than one ability, she had always let her body automatically choose the ink it needed for that moment. It was an involuntary decision—like breathing. Except, this time she forced her body into the state. Her brain was wired to protect her body and let her know when things were off.

She turned her eyes to her fiancé, who was frozen in place. Watching her.

"It picked Alicia's," she said softly. "Not the healing power that she's using now, but the original. How her tatù got started. As a diagnostician. It told me..." A hand slipped down to her belly, and her entire body seemed to be deciding how best to protect the little life inside her. "Devon...it told me that I'm p-pregnant."

He didn't blink. Didn't even breathe.

Neither did the others.

Not a single person on the porch of the London house moved a muscle as Rae stood before them at the door. She stared at their faces. Wide-eyed and motionless. Rigid as a trio of beautiful statues, with her fiancé standing right at the front.

"I didn't plan it," she added hastily. "It's certainly not something that I had in mind. I mean, you and I are supposed to get married now—not get pregnant. And I know exactly what you're thinking: *no way* can we have a child with things the way they are right now. Especially after tonight."

Her whole body tightened in anticipation, clenching her hands tightly together, as she stared up into Devon's eyes. She was so close that she could see every fleck of gold around the irises. Every last drop of the glowing sunset as it clung to his long lashes.

"But the thing is..." her eyes searched his, gazing up imploringly," I think—no, I know—that I really *want* this child. *Your* child. A child who would be a little of you, and a little of me. A child we could raise together. Love together. Teach how to read..." Her voice trailed off as she dropped her eyes to the ground.

She, Devon, Molly, and Julian hadn't said much since departing the royal wedding just a few hours earlier. They had said even less on the way back from Privy Council building, after finishing what had to be one of the longest debriefings in the history of the PC. They hadn't talked at all the entire car ride back to London, and they didn't say a word now as they stood on the porch in bloodied ball gowns and tuxedos. She hadn't argued at the Council table that she was the president. Bile rose at the back of her throat. She didn't want the title.

The realization didn't come as a shock. She wanted a maternity leave.

At this moment, however, the stage belonged to Rae. But she didn't for the life of her know what to do with it.

"I guess what I'm trying to say is...I love you. I love you enough to want to spend the rest of my life with you. And I'm going to love this child." A flush of fear came over her, and she ended in a quiet, faltering voice. "My only hope is that...y-you're going to love him—or her—too."

There was only so long she could avoid looking at him. Only so long she could avoid looking at all of them. A shiver trembled her hands as she pulled in a deep breath and lifted her eyes.

A sea of blank faces stared back at her. Blank faces and rigid bodies.

They were still standing exactly where they'd frozen when she first turned around. When she'd first thrown up her hands and made her impromptu, tear-filled confession.

The breeze picked up, and the soft hum of a car engine echoed down the street as Mrs. Ava Milton, their next-door neighbor, rounded the corner in her aging Mercedes.

Rae's shoulders wilted as she let out a long sigh. "And *that's* how I would tell you...if I ever got up the courage."

A numbing kind of dread settled in the pit of her stomach as she took her place at the front of the line and twitched her fingers towards the sky. Her father's tatù kicked into effect and, just like that, the thin veil of time she'd been holding back sprang free, releasing its hostages.

"—actually had the nerve to ask what I was doing there!" Molly snapped. She couldn't know it at the time, but she'd actually started the sentence five minutes earlier. "Like he couldn't possibly fathom what someone like me would've been doing on a PC mission. Someone like *ME!*"

Julian rubbed his eyes, looking extremely tired. It was a look he hadn't been able to shake since the dozens of sniper dots finally vanished from his body. It was the same look of exhaustion through the interrogation, still holding as he'd dragged himself back to house from the car. "Because you're pregnant."

A soft gasp erupted out of Rae. She spun around, hesitating just as Julian finished his response.

"—He was probably just concerned, Molly. Your belly's showing."

Before Molly could retort Devon spoke up as well, reaching for his keys. "It's true. The Privy Council has one of the highest-working mortality rates of any agency in Europe. That includes the Center for Infectious Diseases and the bomb squad. There's a reason they don't tend to employ women who're expecting. Let alone send them out into the field."

Molly put her hands on her hips, shaking back her long crimson hair. While interrogations tended to make the others guarded and stressed to the point of physical exhaustion, they revved her up. Filling her with an aggressive sort of zeal the others had learned to avoid after such debriefings. "Well, that's just sexist and completely unacceptable," she fired back, looking for an argument from her favorite men when, clearly, all they wanted to do was sleep. One hand slipped down to her belly, and her eyes flashed fiercely. "I'm pregnant, not handicapped! And I'll be dammed if some high and mighty council of *men* tells me when I have to stop working."

Her words rang out angrily in the crisp evening air, and when the boys merely held up their hands in a ceasefire, unwilling to engage, she turned to Rae instead. "Kerrigan, back me up here. You're the president, after all."

Rae jerked back to the present, trying to remember the question. She was staring at Devon, completely riveted as he searched obliviously for his keys. "I'm sorry...what?"

Molly rolled her eyes with an impatient *huff*. "I was saying that pregnancy is a *blessing*, not a curse. We can still have babies and continue on with the rest of our lives, right? It's not like the sky is going to fall."

Did she just...? Is she really asking...? Okay, breathe. Just breathe. Instead, Rae froze in place. White as a sheet. Unable to respond.

The others may have been slightly preoccupied with the fact that they had almost been unceremoniously executed at a royal wedding, but Rae's thoughts were slightly more introverted than that. Ever since she'd pressed her hand against her crystalized dress, felt through the sparkling fabric to the magic getting started just beneath, she hadn't been able to think about anything else.

My debriefing must've been a nightmare for Keene. Who knows what I even said?

When she got neither support nor opposition, Molly gave up and slipped under Julian's arm, leaning sleepily against his chest. "Whatever. I'll just continue to fight these social injustices all on my own. Like a true champion..."

Julian wrapped his arms automatically around her, resting his chin on the top of her head though his tired eyes stayed fixed on the wall. "Give 'em hell, sweetie."

"I think I will."

Devon sighed inaudibly and pushed open the door. "Knock yourself out, Skye. Tomorrow, I'm with you. Tonight, I'm just looking for a bed—"

But that wasn't meant to be.

The second the door opened, the gang was attacked all over again.

"THEY'RE HERE!" a painfully shrill voice screeched onto the landing, making Rae's eyes blink in shock and suddenly focus right there on the spot. "ANTHONY, THEY'RE HERE! TRIS!"

The gang shrank backwards in astonishment as Commander Fodder, Beth, Tristan, Luke, and Angel came rushing out onto the porch, colliding with the gang. They attacked like a well-intentioned swarm; grabbing onto any unbruised, undamaged bit of skin they could find to pull the others inside, slamming the door safely behind them in the process.

What the hell?!

Before Rae could say a single word, she was swept off her feet. She let out a gasp of surprise, but the others were having similar luck. Her head jerked back and forth like a rag doll as she was passed around, accosted at every turn by questions and demands and soothing hands, before ending up in the crushing embrace of her mother.

A mother who seemed entirely incapable of releasing her, despite the fact that worried little trails of smoke were spiraling up from her trembling hands.

"Mom." She tried to make herself heard over the deafening din of voices, tapping Beth on the shoulder as she struggled to breathe. "Mom, you're setting my coat on fire..."

It was no use. Beth was in her own world. Completely out of reach.

And from the looks of things, she wasn't the only one.

"Dad, I'm fine." Devon was trying to casually extract himself from his father's grasp, but Dean Wardell was holding on just as tightly as Beth. In fact, judging by the slightly bluish tint to his son's lips, it might have been even harder. "Seriously, I'm okay. You can let go."

He might as well have saved his breath. Tristan simply closed his eyes and crushed his son against him, gripping a fist of his jacket and a fist of his hair.

Just behind him, Molly was being gently attacked by both Luke and his father. One held her tenderly in his arms, burying his face in her fiery curls, while the other looked her up and down with the practiced eye of a seasoned general, checking for any and all damages.

"You're sure you're all right?" the commander asked urgently, hovering in a tight circle. "I can have the Knights' doctor here in less than an hour to check on you and the baby."

"I'm fine, Commander Fodder. Really, it's—" She broke off with a little gasp as Luke suddenly lifted her off the floor. He didn't seem to notice it himself. "I...I promise."

Fodder nodded automatically, but it didn't register. Instead, he whipped out his phone. "I think I'll give her a call. See if she's in the area."

"No, that's really all right. If I could just get some..." she trailed off as her shoes clattered to the floor, turning to Luke instead. "Uh, honey? You know I'm in the air, right?"

Julian and Angel said not a word as they came together in the center of the floor. They simply embraced. Staring so deep into each other's eyes, Rae could swear they could read minds.

Okay...we obviously missed a step...

The only person who hadn't rushed forward was Gabriel.

He was in the kitchen, a little farther back. But he looked no less anxious. The second the four of them had stumbled inside, he slowly lowered his mug of coffee and took a step forward.

Green eyes locked onto blue as he and Rae shared a long look.

"Are you all right?" he said softly. His voice was intentionally lost amongst the clamor of the crowd, but they both knew that Rae could hear him.

"I'm fine," she whispered, peering out over her mother's shoulder as Beth's tears tangled in her raven hair. "I'm fine."

"That's not what they told us." Beth clutched her impossibly tighter, thinking her daughter had been speaking to her. "They told us that you were last seen being dragged into a room. That the door closed and no one else could get to you. That there was gunfire..." She broke off with a shudder, unable to say the rest. Around the room, her silent terror was reflected in the faces of everyone else who had been left behind. Staring at their phones. Bracing themselves for the worst. Powerless to do anything except wait.

The gang shared a fleeting look as they suddenly understood.

"I'm sorry," Rae murmured, slipping into a strength tatù to gently ease away. "We were taken straight to a debriefing, but someone should have called you. We didn't know you hadn't heard anything at all, or else I would have called myself."

The words were heartfelt, but they had little effect on the other people in the room. It was as if merely seeing that the four of them were alive was no longer enough. They had to feel it. They had to prove it. Anything to make the nightmare of the last few hours go away.

"You're bleeding," Tristan murmured, pulling back to examine Devon's neck. In a blur of speed he tilted his son's head, only to discover the injection site. A strange stillness came over him, and his face darkened with a look of scarcely controlled rage. "What happened to you?"

Devon stared back helplessly, completely at a loss as to what to do.

And he wasn't the only one.

On the other side of the room, Molly was being lovingly accosted. Luke had yet to release her from his arms, but the commander had managed to force them both down into a chair. While his son merely gripped onto the tiny girl like his life depended on it, Fodder carefully slid a hand in between to take her pulse, moving so casually it was like he hoped they wouldn't notice.

Luke didn't. Molly most certainly did.

"Guys, I'm..." She craned her neck upwards, choking slightly on a lock of Luke's golden brown hair before cartoonishly spitting it from her mouth. "I told you, I'm—"

"Let me see that."

Angel and Julian had finally broken their silent embrace, and she was perched on a stool to get a better look at the gash running along the side of his head. He was clearly in no mood to be coddled, but she just as clearly wasn't taking no for an answer. "It doesn't look terribly deep..." she murmured under her breath.

"I told you," Julian inserted quietly.

"...but I'm still going to clean it out. In the meantime, Gabriel can fix your wrist."

Julian stiffened in dismay as she vanished into the kitchen, only to be replaced immediately by her brother. Most people would have taken the swap. But, ironically enough, given the personality of the brother in question, Julian didn't have much more leeway than he did with Angel. "It's fine," he muttered half-heartedly, cradling the arm in question against his chest. "I don't need any help."

Gabriel nodded briskly. "Do you want me to tell her that? Or would you prefer to do it yourself?"

There was a beat of silence.

Then Julian reluctantly extended his arm.

Rae looked away before she could see the snap that followed. Before she could hear the muffled cry. It was a running joke with the gang that there was rarely a day when at least one of them wasn't covered in somebody else's blood. And somebody else's were the good days. Most of the time, they were covered in their own.

It was a testament to how long they'd been living under those bizarre conditions that she hadn't even noticed what a bedraggled bunch they were until they got home. Until they were contrasted sharply against the others who'd been waiting in the living room.

It doesn't help that we're in black tie, she thought sullenly as her mother began going over every inch of skin with the unyielding efficiency of a battlefield medic. *Blood always looks worse in black tie.*

"Dad, please. Enough."

Rae glanced over, her arms lifted obediently out to her sides, to see Devon still trying to escape the concerned grasp of his father.

By now, the dean had somehow removed Devon's jacket and was examining a cut on his shoulder with a paternal frown. "What happened here?" He completely ignored his son's requests and focused on the wound, expertly prodding around the edges to judge the depth.

Devon flinched painfully and bit down on his lip. "I got grazed by a bullet," he admitted under his breath, still trying to tug himself free. "It's not a big deal, all right? Nothing actually—"

Tristan held him steady, forcing Devon to look him in the eyes. "You got grazed by a bullet as someone fired a gun at you. But it's not a big deal. Right."

Devon held his gaze for only a second before looking away with a flush. The mere concept of his father expressing any sort of parental concern for him was still completely foreign to him. He didn't know how to handle it on the best of days, let alone while suffering from mild blood loss.

His eyes flew desperately around the room before finding his fiancée's. He held them there for a moment, a silent cry for help. But Rae was in the exact same boat herself.

"And what about this?" Beth muttered, sweeping her daughter's hair back to look at a severe discoloration snaking up the back of her neck. "Honey, this looks like the imprint of a boot—"

Rae sighed, trying her best to keep it together. "I'm sure that was there before."

Beth's eyes narrowed as the poorly-timed joke died in the air between them. "Rae Kerrigan, up until ten minutes ago I was under the impression you were dead." Her voice was flat and expressionless, yet carried a haunting weight at the same time. "Given that information, I'm sure you'll find it in your impatient heart to allow your *mother* the time she needs to see you safe and alive."

Rae gulped and nodded, dropping her eyes to the floor in silent surrender.

All around the room, her friends were doing the same thing.

They stood there quietly. Letting themselves be fussed over, and coddled, and prodded until the collective heartbeat of the room returned to normal. Once it had, they remained were they were as the process repeated itself. Several more times.

Finally, when the day's overwhelming fatigue was threatening to drop them where they stood, Molly pulled out the pregnancy card.

"I think I should probably get to bed," she said cautiously, gazing around with wide eyes as she lowered a deliberate hand to her belly. "We've all had a *really* long day…"

It was kind of her to use the plural, including the others in their plan. Their heads snapped up and they looked around as well, almost afraid to hope as the others silently conceded the point.

"Of course," Fodder said quickly, taking a step back as Luke swept Molly off her feet. "We'll pick back up in the morning. You can see the doctor then."

Only Rae, Devon, and Tristan could hear her mumble, "Can't wait" as she was carried off to bed.

When the dean realized how tired they all were, he bowed his head apologetically and turned to his son. "I'm sorry," he said softly as Julian and Angel breezed past on their way upstairs. "I didn't mean to overstep, I just…" His voice tightened and he made a visible effort to keep steady. "I've just never been so afraid in my entire life."

It was this moment of quiet honesty that broke through to Devon.

His lips parted in surprise as a very peculiar expression flickered across his face. For a second, he merely stared. Then he stepped forward and gave his father a tight hug.

Would you look at that? Miracles do happen.

Now it was Tristan's turn to be surprised. His face went white with it before warming with a radiant smile as his arms slowly came down to complete the embrace. "I love you, Devon," he murmured into his son's hair. Softer than a whisper. More powerful than if he'd shouted it. "You know that, right?"

Devon nodded silently, gripping harder onto his father's coat. When he finally stepped back, he looked almost as shaken as his father.

"Can we find a minute to talk in the morning?" he asked quietly. "Before you head back?" A little tremor ran through his hands, and he nervously smoothed them flat. "I wanted...I wanted to tell you something."

Rae's eyes widened as the dean gave his son a reassuring smile. Rae made a mental note to start calling him Tristan. Not just Dean Wardell.

The dean—Tristan nodded again. "Of course. Anything you like."

With that the men parted, having both reached their emotional limit for the day. Devon flashed Rae a fleeting grin as he headed up the stairs, cocking his head towards the bedroom. She nodded once, and returned her attention to Beth.

They were the only two people left standing. And while Rae was hyper-aware of it, staring at her mother with a tender smile, Beth was still in her own little world.

"Well, that should do it..." she murmured, looking her daughter up and down. "I mean, it's not to the level of quality that I'd like, but..."

For the last twenty minutes she'd cleaned, and sterilized, and braced, and bandaged to her heart's content. Reaching out her hand automatically as her daughter patiently conjured her enough medical supplies to service an entire platoon. No cut was too small to escape her attention. There wasn't a single bruise that didn't demand her immediate focus and care.

By the time she was finished, Rae looked like some kind of incomplete mummy. One that people had begun wrapping, but had given up on halfway through.

"Mom," she began slowly, holding out her arms with a hidden smile, "I'm going to go to bed now, all right? So that you can get back to the asylum with the rest of the crazy people."

Half an hour ago, that joke would have gotten her an extra splash of rubbing alcohol. Now, Beth lifted her eyes with a tired smile.

"I'm sorry, honey." She gave her daughter one last hug, careful to avoid any gauze. "But every mother turns out to be a little crazy. You'll figure that out when you have a child yourself."

Rae's heart skipped a beat, as her stomach dropped down to the floor.

There had been about five minutes. Five minutes where she forgot it was happening. Forgot that her entire world had turned upside-down leaving her spinning in the middle. "Yeah, I...I guess I will."

Beth stroked back her hair, and quickly kissed her on the forehead before going to get her coat. While the commander and Devon's father were staying the night, Beth had apparently left Simon under the supervision of some incredibly jumpy Privy Council guards. She had to get back.

"I'll see you in a few days," she promised. "In the meantime, please try to fight all those awful instincts of yours and *get some rest*. You're going to need it."

Rae paled, instinctively clutching a hand to her stomach. "...I am?"

Beth was too distracted to notice. She simply pulled out her car keys and pushed open the door, glancing back over her shoulder with a chilling smile. "We've got a bad guy to kill."

Rae dropped her hand immediately. Almost relieved to be talking about something normal. "Oh, right. Yeah." She lifted her hand in a farewell wave. "On that note, sweet dreams."

Beth laughed quietly as she vanished up the darkening street. "Sweet dreams."

Rae stood alone in the living room for a long time. Hand on her stomach. Eyes on the road. Every minute or so she would slip back into Alicia's tatù, spreading her fingers tentatively over her abdomen, stunned senseless every time she was greeted with a tiny spark of life.

When the clock on the wall chimed two, she jumped in her skin.

How the hell did that happen?! Have I really been down here that long?!

She rushed up the stairs, slipping back into the fennec fox so as not to disturb anyone, but she needn't have bothered. The house was fast asleep. And when she pushed open the door to her room and gazed down at the bed, Devon was fast asleep, too.

She stared at him for a full minute. Re-memorizing the lines of his face. Soaking in every beautiful detail. Trying to imagine them on a child.

Then a little ball of golden fur wriggled up from in his arms, and she snapped back to the present. Her lips curled up into an automatic smile as she slipped into her pajamas and climbed under the covers. There wasn't a square inch of her body that had escaped her mother's medical assault, and Annie instantly wormed her way over, nibbling curiously at the tips of the gauze.

Rae kissed her gently on the nose before looking back up at Devon. The few streaks of moonlight able to get through their curtains painted silver lines down his face, making him look like some fairytale prince. The kind who'd had an especially rough day, and needed to sleep it off with his girl and his puppy.

The corners of her mouth curled up in a little smile as she slipped her hand into his.

"Devon," she whispered, giving it a gentle squeeze. "Sweetie, wake up."

He stirred faintly, but didn't wake. Sleep had caught him firmly in its grasp, and every bone in his body was heavy with it.

Rae stroked his hair and tried again. "Honey...I need to tell you something."

This time, his eyes fluttered open. He looked around for a second, unsure whether he was asleep or awake, before turning to Rae.

"Did you say something?" he murmured in a disoriented daze. "Is everything okay?"

He could barely get the words out without slurring them, and Rae let out a silent sigh.

This wasn't going to happen tonight.

Tonight had put them through enough.

Maybe tomorrow?

"Everything's fine," she whispered, giving him a quick kiss on the lips. "I didn't say anything. Go back to sleep."

He stared dazed for another split second before nodding slowly as his head sank back into the pillow. His eyes fluttered heavy, then shut. And a few seconds later, he was asleep.

"I just thought you might want to know..."

Rae lay back on the mattress beside him, both hands clutched tightly across her stomach.

"...I'm pregnant."

Chapter 2

Devon wasn't beside her when Rae woke the next morning. She groped around blindly for him on the sheets, and came up empty. Then an over-excited puppy jumped onto her face.

"Annie!" she gasped, extinguishing the ice blue flames that had sprung immediately from her hands. "You scared me!"

There comes a point after enough people have tried to kill you that you start to develop certain habits. Lethal little reflexes like conjuring a grenade, only to discover that the 'intruder in the garden' was actually the mailman.

Or accidentally setting the mattress on fire when surprised.

Rae held up the dog with one hand, using a handy water tatù to put out the flames with the other. When she was finished, nothing but a soggy scorch mark remained.

"Sorry about that," she murmured as she and the puppy stared down at it. At the same time, they tilted their heads speculatively to the side. "Guess it's a good thing you're here. I only have a few months to stamp those instincts out of me..." She trailed off, feeling suddenly lost, then the puppy licked the entire length of her face. Her lips curved up into a wide grin, and she held it still long enough to plant a kiss on its forehead. "That's the spirit. We can train each other."

Annie yipped cheerfully in response.

With a giggle, Rae forgot about the problems of the present and dropped the puppy back onto the bed, rolling the two of them all over the mattress as they began to play.

She hadn't realized it when she got Annie, but there was something delightfully therapeutic about spending time with something so innocent. Something so prone to fits of uncontrollable joy and tempered with blinding, unconditional adoration. She could see why Devon was so taken with her. It was addictive, that kind of release. Like coming up for air after a long day.

She wondered if a child would be the same way...

Secretly thrilled with the idea she redoubled her efforts, crouching down with a playful growl as Annie pulled herself up to her full height, puffing out her little chest like a lion. Rae countered by conjuring a bouquet of flowers, driving the dog crazy as she dangled them just out of reach. Annie promptly retaliated by throwing up the handful of treats Rae conjured as well.

The two of them had just locked into a ferocious game of tug-of-war, featuring Devon's favorite shirt, when the door opened and Molly swept inside.

"*Finally*, you're awake!" She dropped down onto the bed beside them, running her fingers back through her perfect hair as if she'd already had a rather trying morning. "I need some back-up here; the boys are getting out of control."

Annie hiccupped and then snorted. Tail wagging, she stopped moving long enough to give Molly a cheerful bark. Rae sat up against the headboard with a smile.

"Oh yeah? And what might the boys be doing?"

Molly started to answer, then stared with a worrisome expression at the dog. "You're not, like...trying to poison her, are you?"

Rae glanced over, then shook her head. "I tried to conjure her some treats. Might have been a few too many. She'll be right as rain in no time."

"You didn't," Molly said chidingly. She snapped her fingers and the puppy dove into her lap, staring up with an adorably martyred expression. "Rae Kerrigan, how many times do we have to tell you? Stick to drugs, dresses, and drinks. How dare you turn your evil onto this poor dog."

As undignified as it was, even she had to grin as Annie leapt up and planted a huge, wet kiss on the side of Molly's neck, effectively destroying her carefully selected blouse in the process.

"We might have to get one of these," she murmured, shooting little sparks into the air for Annie to chase. "Something for the baby to play with…"

Rae looked up with a start. Four minutes, this time. It had only been four minutes that she'd forgotten about the fact that her own life was never going to be the same. "Do you think that would work?" she asked innocently, trying to keep the rabid curiosity from her voice. "Do puppies do well with kids?"

Molly shrugged. "Some of them certainly do. We had a dog growing up. Granted it was bred to fit inside a handbag, so I'm not sure how much damage it could actually do."

Rae stifled a grin. Of course it was. She was also willing to bet that the poor animal had been the victim of all baby Molly's first ventures into the realm of styling and cosmetics.

"At any rate, we'll have Julian looking ahead every step of the way."

It was like a lightbulb went off inside Rae's head. Filling her with almost painful relief while simultaneously stopping her heart with the utmost dread.

Oh crap! Julian! She forced a tight smile onto her lips and kept watching Molly. *This is going to be like the engagement all over again! How could I be so stupid?!*

As Molly continued babbling on about how she fully intended to take advantage of their friend's clairvoyant power Rae's eyes flew to the door, staring with such intensity she was surprised she couldn't see through it and all the way down the hall.

He's going to see it! If he hasn't already. Crap! He's going to find out before I can even tell Devon!

"Molls," she interrupted suddenly, "is Devon downstairs?"

Molly paused long enough to pull in a breath. "No, he went out with his dad on a walk this morning. I was going to try to follow along and eavesdrop, but they looked *super* serious, so I went back inside."

Rae leaned back against the headboard, staring with a worried frown at the bed. "That was very noble of you."

Molly nodded cheerfully, then continued on with her one-sided spiel. The monologue had now shifted to the topic of children's play clothes. There was a chance it could go on for hours.

He won't even mean to see, it'll just happen. There's no way to stop it. It's a miracle he hasn't already. Or maybe he has...

Rae pulled her knees up to her chest with a thoughtful stare, nodding whenever it seemed appropriate to punctuate the unending stream of talking from the other side of the bed.

Her only bit of luck was that Julian had a lot on his mind. After psychically connecting with a homicidal psychopath to see the end of the world, he'd come to... only to find himself staring down the barrel of a gun. It was enough to distract any sane person the following morning.

But, strangely enough, Rae was willing to bet that's not what had him so aloof and distracted.

He hadn't been the same since finding out about the connection between Simon and his father. Since the day he'd gone on a rampage through the house, only to come to physical blows with his best friend.

It was like getting just a glimpse into the tragedies of his past made them all the worse. After all, this was a man who could literally see anything. Whose unlimited access to the past, present, and future put entire worlds at his fingertips. He had grown unfamiliar with mere glimpses and half-truths. He needed the entire story. Needed to know what had happened, from start to finish.

So that he could get some kind of closure. So he could begin to move on.

"—which led me to question the exact nature of a 'romper,' but it's..." Molly trailed off suddenly, staring down in alarm. "Rae, what the hell happened to your bed?"

Rae snapped out of her trance to follow her friend's gaze. Aside from the watery scorch mark burned into the center of the mattress, the entire thing was plastered with random bits of tape and gauze, discarded souvenirs from Beth's efforts the previous evening.

"Oh..." Rae glanced down at her arms in surprise. Little Annie must have had a busy night, because there wasn't a single bandage left intact. "That's...I can explain that."

Molly's eyebrows lifted as she gave her friend a suspicious look. "Are you and Devon getting into some weird bondage thing you haven't told me about?"

A scarlet blush heated Rae's cheeks as she hurried to pick up the pieces. "No! We're not into—"

"Who's into bondage?"

The girls looked up as Angel breezed into the room, looking like she'd fallen straight down from heaven just to talk about sexual fetishes. She tossed back her white hair and perched beside them on the mattress, cocking her head to the side with a sparkling smile.

It never ceased to amaze Rae how such stunning contrasts could exist in a single person.

To start, Angel was *beautiful*. And not in a casual way. Not like when you'd flip through a magazine and stare briefly at the faces of the lovely girls inside. But in a way that was impossible to forget. That earned an instant place in your memory. Searing itself into your mind.

There was a lightness about her. From her ivory skin, to her sapphire eyes, to her slender, delicate frame. Right down to her tinkling laughter. The girl was a nymph. A little fairy princess.

But for every bit of lightness, there was darkness there as well.

Angel didn't laugh at the same things as the rest of them. Basic humor was often lost, while the things she found amusing were strange and sometimes cruel. That delicate frame was as lethal as it was lovely. Rae had seen her end a man's life with the mere touch of her hand.

And it took only a breath for those twinkling eyes to go cold. For all the light to die out, leaving nothing but a geographically misplaced assassin in its wake.

And yet...there was Julian.

The love between them wasn't just inspiring, it was transformative. With a single kiss, Angel had seen one door close while another opened in its place. Showing her a future she never knew she could have. A life she'd never even known she wanted.

He was the only thing in the world who could make those eyes go tender. Who could soften the disjointed exterior to a point where she could actually thaw. Where she would actually try.

And she did try. In her own, neurotic way.

Still, it was impossible sometimes not to wonder, if it hadn't been for Julian, whether Angel would have died back at the factory. Fighting for the other side.

That's the same thing you could say about Gabriel, Rae chided herself. *If he hadn't fallen in love with me, he would've killed me instead. Me and all of my friends.*

It was with a smile that she greeted their resident sociopath, watching with silent eyes as Angel perched cheerfully upon the mattress and started playing with her dog.

"Jules and I tried that," she said conversationally, flipping the puppy over. "Bondage, I mean. It turned out different than we thought."

Leaving them to stew in that unsettling thought for a moment, she looked up with a smile.

"Actually, that's what I came here to talk to you about. You know his birthday's coming up in a few weeks, and I wanted to do something special. Something more than just my usual sex him into a coma sort of thing." She misinterpreted the looks on their faces entirely, and hurried to correct herself. "Of course, we'll do that, too—"

"Enough!" Rae held up her hand. "We don't need to hear about all of that." On her other side Molly shook her head at the mattress, pursing her lips to hide a smile.

Angel nodded swiftly, and pushed her hair behind her ears. "Anyway, I tracked down a first-edition book of poems by Alfred, Lord Tennyson. His favorite."

Rae leaned back in surprise. She had been expecting a bazooka. A parachute. A mythological creature that incinerated anything it touched. At any rate, she hadn't known Tennyson was Julian's favorite poet.

"There's a handwritten inscription inside, and Jules is going to love it."

"How the hell are you going to pay for something like that?" Molly blurted. "It has to be thousands and thousands of pounds, and I thought Cromfield tied up all your money—"

Rae pinched her hard in the side, but Angel didn't seem to mind. She gazed at the redhead for a moment, then turned back to the dog. "I've been working on it for a long time," she said simply.

Molly blushed, and stared down at the bed as Rae graciously rescued the conversation.

"So what did you want to talk about?" she asked kindly. "I think the book's a great idea."

She had spent enough time with Angel over the last few months to have grown incredibly attached, despite her rather strange proclivities. They two had bonded more than Rae sometimes realized, and one way or another it was clear to see the girl was trying.

Angel nodded again then fiddled nervously with her hair, looking uncharacteristically uncertain. "The thing is, the seller won't take cash. And that's all I have. He wants a check."

Her lovely face darkened with frustration and, unless Rae was imagining it, the slightest hint of shame. To have her brilliant birthday surprise thwarted by the fact that she'd been raised by a psychopath, beneath a cemetery, without access to a bank account.

Rae and Molly melted at the same time. As capable and exasperating as Angel could be, moments like this made it impossible not to feel utterly protective of her at the same time.

"What can we do?"

Much to everyone's surprise, it was Molly who asked the question. Rae cast her a sideways grin as Angel lifted her head with a tentative smile.

"If I give you the cash, will you write him a check?"

Molly nodded soundly. "I'll do one better than that. After we pick this thing up, I'll take you to my bank and we can set up an account for you there as well."

She clearly thought it was a brilliant idea, but Angel dimmed a little at the thought. Rae swooped in for the save. "I think...we should probably take things one step at a time." While she was sure that Angel could produce enough of the necessary documents to get past bank security, she wasn't sure if any of them were remotely valid. "You know, stick to activities that don't require a passport or birth certificate."

Angel scoffed good-naturedly, pushing to her feet. "Rae, if you don't think I have a passport, you've massively underestimated me. I have twelve."

She made no mention of the birth certificate.

Rae flashed her an easy grin, but grew thoughtful as she watched Angel sweep back down the hall. It wasn't until she'd reached her own bedroom door that Rae called out to her once more. "Hey, Angel. This is really sweet. What you're doing for Jules. It's...it's a good thing."

She didn't want to appear condescending. That's the last thing in the world she wanted. But she didn't want the moment to go unnoticed, either. It was a positive step. She was proud.

Angel paused in the doorway, and tossed back her long white hair. "Well, when you love someone, it's the simplest thing in the world, right?" Her eyes softened with a fleeting smile. "Seize every day. Don't waste a single moment."

The other girls froze behind her as she pushed obliviously through the door.

"Or so my books on human behavior tell me..."

It wasn't until the door swung shut that Molly and Rae turned back to each other, staring with wide, disbelieving eyes.

"She never says what I think she's going to say," Molly muttered incredulously. "Never."

Rae didn't move. She was still staring at the door.

"A first edition Tennyson. Handwritten inscription." Molly lay back on the bed, scooping Annie up to dance her around. "Do you think she robbed a bank?"

Rae's eyes glowed as she stared down the hallway. "You know what? I think her gift is that she didn't."

Rae didn't end up going down for breakfast with the others. When Annie barked and cried to go on a walk, she handed her off to Luke instead. In a rather strange turn of events, she had found inspiration in the most unlikely of places.

And she wasn't going to let that inspiration go to waste.

"Rae?"

She sat straight up on the bed as Devon's voice echoed up the stairs. "I'm up here!"

A second later, far too fast to be plausible, he appeared in the doorway. There was a strange flush to his skin, and a glowing smile stretched across his face. "I did it," he said before she could even ask. "I told my dad we were getting married."

Rae pulled in a quick breath and nodded, trying desperately to keep the words inside. All day she'd been waiting for him to get back, never abandoning her post on the bed, never faltering in her courage. She had completely forgotten about Devon's epic walk with his dad.

"It was just...perfect." He fell on the bed beside her, automatically avoiding the scorch mark without having the presence of mind to ask where it came from. "It went exactly the way that it was supposed to have gone. You know, if we were a normal family."

It wasn't often that Rae heard Devon wax on about being normal. Out of everyone in the gang, he was the one most taken with the fact that they had the ability to stand out. It wasn't until very recently, until he and Rae got serious, that he'd ever considered another option. And even now, Rae was pretty certain that his idea of a 'normal, married life' involved some sort of torpedo-launcher in the garage.

That's okay. Mine does, too.
...right next to the baby stroller.

"Dev, that's wonderful!" she gushed. "I'm so happy for you!"

Devon flashed her a grin before settling back on the bed. His eyes danced and glowed as he remembered, folding his hands behind his head as he stared up at the ceiling with that same smile. "He asked me when it was going to be, and I told him as soon as possible. He even asked me if you were pregnant." He let out a short laugh. "If that's why we were doing it so quickly."

Rae's blood ran momentarily cold, and she glanced at him out of the corner of her eye. "Well, it's not a totally outrageous question—"

"No, of course it isn't! That's the point!" Devon was on his feet again before she could stop him. Before he even noticed that she was reaching out to take his hand. "Everything about it was perfectly normal, Rae. He asked all the right questions. Said all the right things. Like...normal *parent* things to say. He's never really done that before. Not since I was a kid." He chuckled again, running his hand through his hair as he paced in front of the dresser. "Asking if you were pregnant, I almost lost it right there..."

Rae pulled in a sudden breath and sat bolt upright on the bed, making up her mind right then and there. There wasn't going to be some big reveal. No onesie embroidered with 'future little fox,' or ultrasound picture tucked inside his wallet. Angel was right.

When you loved someone, it was simple. There was no time to waste.

"Devon...I'm pregnant."

Chapter 3

Rae wiggled her fingers under the blanket, worried she'd accidentally used her father's tatù and frozen time again. Devon hadn't moved an inch since she told him. He hadn't even breathed.

"...Devon?"

He came out of it with an almost silent gasp, jerking back to life like he had indeed been stuck by some invisible force. Or a time freeze. His eyes were enormous, wider and more dilated than Rae had ever seen them. One foot was still raised an inch or two off the floor to complete the step he'd been taking.

But still, he said nothing.

It was like he was waiting for something. For her to retract it. Or deny it. Or laugh. Or simply finish the sentence in a way that would make the whole thing make sense.

Thoughts raced through her head. Suddenly she was sixteen again, in her second year at Guilder, in love with Devon. She had a feeling she was about to actually freeze time as she played the memory back through her head. They were in Devon's dorm room, and Rae had tried out Desiree's tatù. They'd been kissing, things were building up, and the conversation turned into an argument. She wanted more, but he apparently had to pull the responsibility card and stop the action. She bit her lip as she remembered...

What had she said to him? *What's wrong with messing around a little?*

He had held her and told her he wanted to take things slowly. Then she'd confessed to him that she'd used Desiree's tatù. He'd laughed at first and then started pacing the room, mumbling about not ready to be a father, not ready to have the Council find out. What else had he worried about? How people would react? Treat them? Treat their make-believe child? The danger they would put themselves in?

The memory raced through her head. She'd pressed him. Asked him if he was scared of her. Wondered if she was the result of his worst fears. The evil of two tatùs mixed together.

They'd argued if children were born evil. Or if evil was a result of one's environment. Devon had broken her heart a little that day when he said there could be a gene that predisposed them to do wrong. And that environment could be what brought out their wickedness—or kept it tucked away.

She held her breath as she remembered what she'd said back to him. *"So, logically, if one day we got married and decided to have children, our child would most likely be good—look at you and me! Even if there's a hint of my father's genes, he or she could still be a normal, happy person."* Hadn't she spent most of her life terrified she was suddenly going to turn into her father? To simply wake up one day and have morphed into a monster overnight?

Could that happen to their baby?

Rae shook her head slightly, focusing on the man she loved standing in front of her. The one who was going to convince her that everything was going to be all right.

But yet, he said nothing.

He was waiting for her.

When she didn't react or say anything else, he pursed his lips and tilted his head to the side. His hair spilled across his forehead as he answered with a wordless, "Hmm?"

Okay. Baby steps. Literally.

The poor man was obviously caught in some sort of out-of-body experience, worse than the one she'd just been through.

Rae figured the least she could do was help him find his way out. "I said that I'm pregnant," she said gently, careful not to make any sudden movements as she slowly lowered her feet to the floor. "I found out yesterday at the wedding."

It was impossible to tell how much of this was registering and how much was lost in shock.

"You...you're..." He let out a single gasp of laughter, then went dead quiet. A host of emotions swept across his face before coming up blank. "What do you mean?"

Rae pulled in a trembling breath, and made a concerted effort not to smile. This was going to be one of those moments they remembered for the rest of their lives. She could not go down in history as having laughed aloud while he tried to work it all out.

It's not like I was much better...

"I mean...that you and I are going to have a baby."

If the word *pregnant* wasn't going over, the word *baby* was out of the question. He simply blinked twice, then stared at the mattress, looking like there was a good chance he might pass out.

How is it possible for his skin to be that white? Should I be calling a doctor?

She stood up nervously and reached for his hand. "Sweetie? How...uh...how do you feel about that?"

His head snapped up in surprise. "...Me?" Instead of taking her hand, he reached out behind him—grabbing discreetly onto the wooden dresser for support. "I feel fine about it...I feel—"

That's when he pulled the whole thing down on top of himself.

After digging her fiancé out of a pile of clothing and broken planks, Rae guided him safely to the bed. He followed obediently, floating, as if his feet were still an inch or two off the floor.

It wasn't until he had lain there for a moment—propped up against the headboard—that he shot her a sideways glance. "Sorry about that...I think I was in shock."

Rae pursed her lips. She had said the exact same words after he proposed to her. "That's perfectly understandable."

His eyes dropped down to her belly before slowly lifting back to her face. "You're sure?"

It was the first time he had acknowledged it. The first time he made the connection between her saying the words and something that was actually happening.

She felt her face warm with her radiant smile. "I'm sure. I used Alicia's tatù yesterday after the wedding. I'm...I'm definitely pregnant." Her smile softened sympathetically when Devon simply sat there, his eyes locked on her stomach. After a few seconds of waiting, she leaned down to try to catch his eye. "Rest assured...it's yours."

He looked up in a daze. "...what?"

She shook her head quickly. "Nothing. Bad joke." She reached for him again. This time her fingers slipped into his open hand. "Dev, you need to tell me how you're feeling about this. Because I'm freaking out—"

"How I'm *feeling*?" he interrupted suddenly. She held her breath as his eyes made the slow journey from her belly to her face. Once there, they lingered for a moment before slowly, ever-so-slowly, his face melted into a breathtaking smile. "*Rae.*"

Oh, thank goodness! She dissolved into instant tears. The quiet kind. The happy kind. The kind she couldn't stop as her entire body slumped back against the headboard in unspeakable relief.

But no sooner had she leaned back than she was being moved again. Lifted gently into the air, settling safe inside her fiancé's arms.

"You thought I'd be upset?" he asked incredulously, resting his cheek against her hair.

She wanted to pull back to see him, to watch the continued transformation light up each of his handsome features—one by one. But she was too content just to be held. She didn't realize how *much* she'd needed to be held until that very moment. She thought about the conversation in his dorm room and wondered if he remembered. She smiled. "We've never really talked about it," she murmured, gripping his arms. "...just the hypothetical treehouse conversation. I just didn't...I didn't know if that's something you ever thought about. Something you'd ever actually want."

"Of course I want it." He squeezed her tighter. So tight that she could feel every pounding heartbeat in his chest. "I've always wanted it." A sudden tremor ran through his body, and he pulled back with a nervous laugh. "I'll admit, I never planned on having one quite so soon..."

Rae laughed as well, pushing herself upright as she smoothed down her hair and wiped the remaining tears from her eyes. "Yeah, that's kind of where I'm at, too."

But Devon was no longer present. His entire attention was focused on something else.

His fingers twitched, and he made a compulsive movement towards her before instantly stopping himself. His eyes flashed up and he looked almost shy as he quickly retracted his arm. "I'm sorry...may I?"

It was only then that she realized what he was trying to do. "Devon, of course you can." She rolled up her shirt with a smile. "It's your baby."

He took a second to absorb that, then reached toward her, moving with the speed and caution of someone worried about frightening off a wild animal. Like the tiny human might sense him coming, and run for the hills. Rae bit her lip again, determined not to smile.

He hesitated a split second, hovering half an inch above, then stretched his hand carefully across her stomach, warming her through and through with the very touch. "My baby," he repeated under his breath.

There was a strange possessiveness in the way he stressed the word *my*. A quiet pride in the way he lightly caressed her skin. A flicker of light danced in his eyes before settling into one of the most beautiful smiles Rae had ever seen. Something borderline...paternal.

He is going to be an amazing father.

But all at once, all those warm and tender feelings disappeared. It was like she could actually feel them leave his body. Rushing out with a single breath, leaving a rigid terror in their wake.

"Samantha."

It was softer than a breath. Whispered to himself the way someone would reaffirm a nightmare. Reminding themselves it was real. Reminding themselves it was still coming.

Rae's heart tightened, and her hand clamped down fiercely upon his wrist. "It's going to be fine. We're going to find her, take care of her." When she got no response, she squeezed his hand hard enough to bruise. "Devon, it's going to be fine."

He glanced up for a second, looking not fine at all, then nodded quickly.

With a visible effort, he pushed the nightmare temporarily away. Locking it in some dark corner before turning back to her with a genuine smile.

In a blur of sunshine and speed, he kissed her.

Kissed her stomach. Kissed her lips. Kissed her hands. Kissed every available bit of skin he could find before falling back on the mattress with a bark of euphoric laughter.

Rae gasped at the blinding assault, still trying to catch her breath. "*That* was more of the reaction I was hoping for."

She bit her lip with a grin as he tilted her gently back onto the sheets, propping himself delicately above her. Her shirt was still halfway up her ribs, and it quickly reclaimed his attention.

"I still can't believe this is happening..." He closed his eyes and pressed his lips against her stomach, sending a host of shivers sweeping through her from head to toe. When he opened them again, he was a changed man. "I never knew I could be so happy," he murmured, skating his fingers over her skin. His sparkling eyes flashed up to meet hers. "I never knew one person could make me so happy."

It was all Rae could do to keep herself together. With all the emotion swelling her heart, she thought the thing might burst. "Not one person," she corrected teasingly, "but two."

He leaned back a bit as he considered this, his eyes glassing over as they locked on the bed.

"There will be three of us," he mused. "You, me, and the...the baby," he said the word slowly, trying it out for the first time.

Although he had yet to become fully aware of it, his entire world had just flipped upside-down. And, unlike his fiancée, he didn't have the ability to stop time to work it all out.

"That's right," Rae gushed, unable to contain her excitement. "I'm going to be a mom. And you're going to be a dad."

The words rang out in the quiet room, layered with decades of implication. Devon's smile faded, and he paled so drastically she thought he might pass out on the spot.

Baby steps...

"What the hell is wrong with you?!" Julian exclaimed, struggling to keep his balance as he and Molly were manhandled into the room. Luke and Angel followed curiously behind, watching as their lovers were essentially kidnapped before their very eyes.

"Devon! Take it easy!" Julian barked, his weight resisting against his best friend.

But Devon was a man on a mission. He wasn't going to let his best friend slip away into the future. This was the kind of news he wanted to share himself.

Unfortunately, his ways of keeping Julian in the present left a lot to be desired.

"Hey! OW!" The psychic threw up his hands as he was shoved into a wall, but no sooner had he landed than he was being dragged forward again, thrown carelessly onto the bed. *"Seriously?!"*

Rae had collected Molly with more dignity, but she was no less excited. Even though Rae tended to avoid it, Riley's cheetah tatù slipped to the surface and she found herself bouncing from foot to foot at a near blinding speed.

"Will someone please tell us what the heck is going on?" Molly demanded as she was pushed down next to Julian. "And why you felt the need to interrupt my afternoon meditation."

"You were watching infomercials," Luke countered with a grin as he leaned against the wall by the doorway, clearing content on sticking to the easiest route of escape if needed.

"Precisely."

The edges of Julian's eyes began to automatically whiten, but Devon struck him on the back with enough force to shatter stone. "Oh, no you don't!"

"Wait a minute." Molly shrank back on the bed, brandishing a hairbrush like a weapon. "Is he possessed again? Angel, freeze him! Rae, check him for a knife!"

"I'm *not* possessed," Devon assured her quickly. "I just...*we* just have some news." His eyes flickered to Rae, who stopped bouncing and stared back, trying to stop a smile that kept trying to break through.

"What," Julian sulked, examining a new tear in his jacket, "she's pregnant?"

There was a pause.

"Damn it to hell, Julian!"

Julian's dark eyes flashed up to Devon in shock. "I was kidding! I didn't actually...*Wait.*" His mouth fell open as he glanced between them, unable to believe it was true. "She is?" His head shot back and forth like he was watching a tennis match. "You are?" Head swung again. "Devon, so help me, if you're kidding..." Hair flew to the right. "Rae, if he's taking the mick—Wait, you're actually...pregnant?"

There was an ear-splitting shriek as Molly clapped her fingers over her mouth, then abruptly fell quiet. Staring with impossibly wide eyes.

"As a matter of fact..."

Rae and Devon stepped forward at the same time that Julian and Molly pushed shakily to their feet. For a moment, the four friends simply stared at each other.

Then Rae's hand slipped down to her stomach with a radiant smile. "I am."

It was quiet for only a moment. Then came the explosion.

"WHAT?!"

In a streak of ivory and crimson Molly flew across the room like she had wings, tackling her best friend with a force that made both of the expectant fathers in the room cringe with automatic concern. They tumbled into the remains of the broken dresser, shrieking breathlessly all the while.

"You're *pregnant*?!" she gasped, trapping Rae in a kind of chokehold. "I can't believe it! How far along are you?! How long have you known?!"

From there, she dissolved into one of those signature Molly monologues. Talking only half to Rae, and half to the baby. Doing so at a pitch so impossibly high that the puppy—who had just wandered into the room—bolted right back out of it and down the stairs.

Julian and Devon were only slightly more dignified.

They locked eyes for a moment before coming together in the kind of embrace that made Luke laugh out loud and Angel shake her head, muttering, "I knew it," with a resigned expression.

"Devon..." Julian gasped, still in complete shock, "that's just...I mean..."

"I know." Devon spat out a mouthful of dark hair, grinning ear to ear. "It hasn't even sunk in yet. Rae's acting so calm about it, but I'm just..."

Neither one seemed particularly able to complete a sentence, but it didn't matter. In moments such as these, they had always shared a strange kind of telepathy.

"Yeah. I can imagine."

They held on for a moment longer before pulling away at the same time. Each with the same look of wide-eyed euphoria. Each with something pressing they had to say.

"Congratulations—"

"You have to be the godfather," Devon interrupted in a sudden rush, like if he didn't say it that very moment he might somehow lose his chance. "Please."

Across the room, Rae looked over and caught his eye. The two of them hadn't even discussed it, but as she peered over Molly's shoulder they shared a knowing smile.

Of course Julian would be the godfather. It wouldn't be anyone else.

And on that note...

"Molly," she said softly, slipping into a strength tatù. It was the only way to escape the girl's impossible grasp. "Would you do that, too? Would you be the godmother?"

The high-pitched sermon came to a screeching halt as Molly stared up at her with a pair of enormous, watery eyes. She didn't answer. She simply collapsed into a fit of tears.

At that point, Luke peeled himself off the wall and moved forward with a gentle smile. "She's been doing that a lot lately," he explained kindly. "Blame it on the hormones."

He lifted her up like a small child but she reached out for Rae instead, wrapping her arms tightly around her neck with a strangled sob.

"Yes, of course I will! You know you're going to be the godmother to mine!"

It looked like she wanted to say more, but the tears overtook her again and the others were forced to merely wait, locked in a comical embrace. Luke holding Molly. Molly hugging Rae.

After a few seconds of awkward silence, Luke caught Rae's eye through the waves of scarlet hair, and offered a quiet, "Congratulations. You're going to be incredible."

"Thanks," she whispered as they took alternating turns patting Molly's back. "I still can't believe it's all happening."

He flashed her a knowing smile. "That doesn't go away..."

It was a rather extreme reaction, but on the other side of the room Julian seemed beyond words as well. He simply stared at Devon in shock, nodding with a shy smile. "...I would be honored."

There was a beat of silence then Devon let out a burst of laughter, clapping his friend on the back. His eyes twinkled as the intense emotional moment shattered on the spot. "You'd be *honored*?"

Julian flushed defensively and shoved his arm away. "That's what people say, isn't it? What did you want me to—"

"Just say *yes*, Julian."

"Fine. Yes," he snapped. But it only took a few seconds for his glare to lighten up into a brotherly grin. Then a curious one. "Why did you try to beat me up on the way in here?"

"I know you have a hard time trancing out when you're in pain," Devon replied cheerfully.

Julian blinked. "You could have just asked me not to."

A look of surprise lightened Devon's face as he considered the notion for the first time. "I honestly didn't think of that."

Rae watched the entire exchange from the other side of the room, and snorted with muffled laughter. She was about to put in her two cents when a pair of slender arms wrapped around her waist. By the time she even registered the embrace, Angel was already pulling away.

"So I'm guessing you're not going to tell Gabriel about this either?"

A little chill ran up Rae's arms, and she bowed her head with a sigh. The two of them had almost the exact same conversation when Rae got engaged just a few months before. When they were living in the safe house in Scotland, about to battle Cromfield once and for all.

But it isn't the same thing, is it? I know we're gearing up for Samantha, but Gabriel's with Alicia. This kind of thing shouldn't upset him anymore.

"Why wouldn't I?" she asked lightly. "I can tell him and Allie together."

Angel flashed her a look, and she fell silent.

It was easy to say the words. But deep in her heart, Rae knew they weren't exactly true. And one look from his sister confirmed it. "What am I supposed to do, Angel?" she asked softly. "I mean, I don't want to tell a lot of people—certainly not my dad, or anything like that. But it's not like I can hide it forever. I'm going to start to show before long. Am I really supposed to wait until after Samantha—"

"Are you even going to be fighting Samantha?" Angel lifted her eyebrows in surprise. "I would've thought that was completely off the table, given your…news."

On the other side of the room, Devon had gone still. He kept a fixed smile on his face as Julian and Luke bantered back and forth about something to do with children, but his head was tilted to the side in the way it did when he was focusing on something else.

"I…" Rae glanced between them, struggling to come up with a response. "I don't know. We'll cross that bridge when we come to it, I guess."

Devon dropped his eyes to the floor, while Angel gave her a long look. But whatever it was she was looking for, Rae would never know.

In the end, Angel merely flashed a tight smile. "Well, congratulations. That's going to be one lucky kid."

The words touched Rae in spite of herself. In the thousands of random hypotheticals circling constantly through her head, she had never once considered the kid to be lucky.

Beautiful, perhaps. Freakishly gifted beyond the confines of the human world.

But *lucky*? If anything, didn't having two such trouble-magnets for parents put the poor little thing squarely into the other camp?

"Thanks, Angel." She kept her eyes on the girl as she drifted back across the room to Julian's side. He wrapped an arm around her shoulders, still chattering on excitedly with Luke as, slowly, the rest of the room fell into the same, spirited conversation.

All except one.

One man who was standing a few feet away, staring out the window with an unreadable expression. Instead of standing in the center of the circle, accepting his friends' congratulations on becoming a new father.

The baby celebration went on long into the night. Luke ran out to pick up take-out from Molly and Rae's favorite Italian restaurant just before closing and, together, the six friends toasted to the next generation of troublemakers. Four with Champagne. Two with sparkling cider.

The speculations got wilder. The spirited predictions got more and more bizarre.

It wasn't long before the entire evening had digressed into one of those nights that Rae loved so well. The kind where all of her favorite people in the world were sitting around the same fire. Safe from the dangers that hunted them. Relaxed in each other's company. Content to pretend that the world stopped at the front doorstep. That this single night of happiness was all there was.

The only problem was, the picture wasn't quite complete.

It was missing Gabriel, who had gone out with Kraigan that day to help the latter search for his own apartment. After some transparent threats from his little sister, Gabriel had agreed to put his personal differences with the man aside long enough to eliminate him as one of Angel's roommates.

According to Kraigan he had been searching diligently since they arrived in London, but no one could imagine he had made much of an impression with any potential landlords. To be honest, Rae was surprised he hadn't resorted to his usual kidnapping and threats. Gabriel, on the other hand, was charm incarnate. If there was one person who could secure a highly-coveted London property without something so basic as a credit check, it was him.

By now, the two of them were probably at some bar. Drinking shots, terrorizing co-eds, and comparing notes about their deviant pasts.

But the picture was also missing Devon, who had grown more and more aloof as the night progressed. Keeping a smile on his face, he withdrew further and further inside his own head.

Rae wished there was something she could do to stop it but, to be honest, she didn't see what could possibly be said. They both knew the danger they were up against. There was no point denying it. And after what had happened at the wedding, they both knew how immediate that danger was. It was an impossible situation. One with only questions. Not an answer in sight.

At one point he got a text on his phone, which seemed to make thing all the worse. His face tightened imperceptibly as he glanced down at the screen. But before Julian—who was seated beside him—could even notice, he'd already slipped the thing back into his pocket with an easy smile.

But despite her fiancé's troubling reserve, the night still managed to end on a high note.

Molly and Luke had decided to stay over, regardless of the fact that they lived about four minutes away, and were setting up downstairs in one of the guest rooms. Angel and Julian, both pleasantly buzzed with Champagne, couldn't keep their hands off each other and vanished abruptly without a word of goodnight.

Leaving Rae and Devon to walk slowly up the stairs together, hand in hand.

"Julian had better be careful," she teased lightly as they both undressed for bed, "or else he's going to be expecting a child of his own before long."

"He and Angel aren't planning on having kids," Devon said abruptly. Rae looked up with a start, and he quickly clarified. "At least...they aren't planning on it right now. Not remotely."

Rae peeled back the covers with a frown, thinking it over. "Because of Angel?" she guessed quietly.

Having grown up the way she had, it wasn't hard to understand why the girl wasn't exactly eager to be a mom. To be honest, Rae would be surprised if the thought had ever crossed her mind.

"Actually, because of both of them." Devon slipped into bed beside her. "He's been that way ever since I met him. Says the future's too dark. He can't imagine bringing a child into it."

Rae flipped off the lamp, and snuggled down into his arms. "But there's light, too. Jules knows that." A wave of sadness tightened her throat as she shook her head. "I can't imagine a world where Julian never has a child. A guy like him has to."

"I don't know," Devon murmured. "Sometimes I think he has a point."

Rae shot up immediately, pulling herself out of his arms. "What's that supposed to mean?" she demanded. "I hate to break it to you, babe, but it's a little too late to turn back the clock on this one."

"No, no, no—that's not what I meant!" He sat up with her, wrapping an arm around her shoulders as he coaxed her back down. "I just mean...the world's a dangerous place. Our world especially. I can understand how it would give him pause."

Rae's heart was still pounding as she lay back on his chest. "But that's why it's our job to keep it safe," she whispered. "You have to believe that we can do that, Devon. If any two people in the world can make it happen—it's you and me."

His chest fell in a silent sigh, but he kissed the top of her forehead. "I know. I know we can."

Rae nodded, temporarily appeased, but something about his voice left her incredibly unsettled. Left a nagging feeling of doubt that plagued her as she tried to fall asleep.

In hindsight, that's why she shouldn't have been surprised when he disappeared in the middle of the night...

Chapter 4

Rae's eyes snapped open and she gasped.

It was like some sort of internal alarm clock went off. A silent warning that only she could hear. One second, she was fast asleep. The next, she lay wide awake, staring in horror at the empty sheets where the love of her life was supposed to be.

A flash of lightning lit the room and she bolted upright, her eyes darting around. It was an ominous moment, like one from a suspense movie where the music suddenly puts you on the edge of your seat. Except there was no music. And this was real life.

"Devon?" she called softly, well aware that if he was anywhere in the house he would still be able to hear her. "Devon, where are you?"

Nothing. Just a chilling silence. One that shook her to her very core.

Something is not right.

Another flicker of lightning and Rae leapt to her feet, pulling on her bathrobe as she raced out into the hall. It was the middle of the night, just a little past three, but she was hardly surprised when she ran into Angel at the top of the stairs. The girl was dressed in a gauzy black nightgown, one that made her look like some evil princess about to cast a spell.

"Julian's gone," she said without preamble. "I checked the house. He's not here."

The hairs on the back of Rae's neck stood, and she instinctively pulled her robe tighter. "Devon's not here either."

There was another bolt of lightning from outside, followed by a deafening growl of thunder. Followed by a panicked scream from the downstairs. Or a cry. It was something in between.

"Devon?" Rae called.

At the same time Angel cried, "Julian?"

Without stopping to think the two girls took off, neither one bothering to use the steps part of the stairs. In a whirling arc of hair Angel flipped straight over the side of the banister, while Rae ran horizontally across the wall. Both skidded to a stop in the foyer right as Molly came racing down the hall.

"I can't find Luke!" she cried. "At first I thought he might have just run back to the apartment to get something, but he's not answering his cell—"

"Julian and Devon are gone, too," Angel interrupted.

Molly's face paled. Over the last few years, they had learned not to take unexplained disappearances lightly. In their world, they usually implied something far worse to come. "Well..." she floundered, glancing fearfully towards the front door, "maybe they just went out celebrating some more? Headed to a bar for some kind of guys' night out..." She looked like she hardly believed what she was saying.

Rae shook her head. "They would have told us. Or left a note." Her face darkened as she recalled the look on her fiancé's face. "And Devon wasn't in any mood to celebrate...trust me."

A sudden sound made her jump, and she turned around to see Angel gearing up by the front door. She was already wearing a long leather trench coat over her negligée, and was in the process of lacing up the combat boots to match.

"Where the heck are you going?" Rae demanded incredulously, and bit back the last of her comment, *Dressed like that?*

Angel finished with one boot, and started on the other. "I'm going to find Julian."

Rae and Molly exchanged a quick look before the latter stepped forward.

"Angel, we have no idea where they are or when they left. They could be in anywhere in England for all we know."

There was a metallic snap as Angel pull two handguns out of nowhere, loaded them, and slipped them into her coat. "Yeah, well, it beats sitting around here."

She yanked open the door, but Rae shut it again with a burst of wind. "You're on a team now," she reasoned quietly. "We don't just go rushing off in the middle of the night on our own. We need to think. Come up with some kind of plan—"

"Julian and I were awake until just after two; meaning that, if they left immediately after, they'd have an hour head start. I've already called the major airports and bus stations, none of which reported any passengers matching Julian's description—so we can rule them out. Now, given that they didn't take any of their cars, I'm assuming they're either on foot or had to wait a minimum of ten minutes for a cab. In this city, that gives us a seventy-mile radius of where they could be." She delivered the speech in a flat monotone then lifted her eyes, her glare cold. "I wasn't trained to go rushing off in the middle of the night without a plan either. I also wasn't trained to sit around waiting for bad news. Stay here if you like; I'm going to find him." Without another word, she spun around and kicked open the door.

"Wait!" Molly called after her. "Where are you even going to start?!"

Angel whipped something silver out of her pocket as she vanished into the darkness. "I'm going to start by calling my damn brother..."

A second later, she was gone.

Rae and Molly stared after her in silence, watching as the door banged open and shut in the storm. Torrents of icy water streamed inside, illuminated every so often by a flash of electricity, as the two gazed out into the dark. Eventually, Rae used her telekinesis to pull the thing closed.

"This feels different," she said quietly.

Molly jumped like she been startled, then flashed her a questioning look. "What?"

"This." Without thinking, Rae's hand slipped down to her stomach. "It feels different when I don't know where to find him. When I don't know if he's safe."

Molly reached down with a sigh and took her hand. "Yeah. That never goes away."

They waited for what felt like an eternity, pacing the kitchen with tired, sleepless eyes. Angel's confidence might have been inspiring but it was rooted in restless panic, not fact. In this part of the country, seventy miles didn't really narrow it down. And if there was nothing more to go off than that, the best thing they could do was remain where they were. And try to stay calm.

Rae didn't want to worry Molly. She kept thoughts of Samantha in the far corners of mind, refusing to let that thought plant any seed.

Mugs of coffee were conjured and swallowed. Then conjured again. Clothes were put on. Phones plugged into their chargers. Together, the two girls created a silent vigil by the front door, taking turns to walk to the window and keep watch. Every thirty minutes or so they would try calling one of the boys, hoping that something—*anything*—had changed. Each time, it went straight to voicemail.

"I'm going to kill him," Molly finally murmured. It was about five in the morning, and the two of them hadn't spoken for at least an hour. Rae lifted her head and glanced over, brows knit in a silent question. "Luke. I'm going to kill him the second he gets home."

Rae sighed and rested her chin back on her hands. For the last forty-five minutes, her eyes had been trained out the window, gazing sleeplessly into the dark. "I thought we agreed not to use the 'k' word until we knew they were okay."

"Yeah, well, things change." Molly glowered at her mug of coffee. It was full to the top, but had long since gone cold. Still, she refused to put it down. "I can't believe he would do this to me."

"Well, if it's any consolation, I don't think it was his idea." Rae's eyes narrowed as she gazed out at the misty streetlamps. The storm had lessened, but only slightly. The thunder and lightning had subsided, making way for the freezing winter rains.

How much longer was Devon going to pull this crap? This *protect her for her own good* bullshit that tripped them up time after time. Whether he was breaking up with her to give her 'freedom,' or shooting himself up with lethal chemicals for her protection, it always seemed to end the same way.

How many more times would they have to play out the same lesson? How many more nights would she have like this one? Sitting by the window, staring at her phone?

Would it happen after she had the baby? Would they both be waiting by the door?

Because, the thing was, she had a good idea of where he had gone off tonight. At least, she had a pretty good idea of what he had gone off to do.

And it happened to involve a certain psychopath they were all intent on killing. A thought she'd been trying to avoid processing. Now, she was tired and irritated. "It's like he can never let himself get too happy," she murmured, staring down at the couch. "It's like he's always waiting for something to go wrong—"

"*Rae.*"

She looked up sharply at the change in Molly's tone.

"They're here."

Like flipping a switch, the hours of fatigue fell away as the two girls discarded their mugs and blankets and stood side by side in front of the door.

Even through the storm, they could hear the metallic screech of brakes as a car they didn't recognize skidded to a stop on the front lawn. They saw dark silhouettes, and could hear the sound of frantic, hushed voices as the car doors opened and the men made their way inside.

"You ready for this?" Rae asked softly.

Molly's eyes flashed in the storm. "You have no idea."

They were prepared for a screaming fight. For a full-on inquisition—torture, chains, the works. They were prepared to stand their ground until they got a satisfactory explanation. No matter how many painful hours or angry tears that might happen to take.

But all of that would have to wait.

"HE'S NOT BREATHING!"

The door burst open and Devon rushed past them, carrying a limp body in his arms. An ominous trail of red followed along behind. With a violent swoop of his arm, he swept everything off the kitchen table and gently lay the person down.

Four other men rushed in after him. More than had left the house that night.

Rae and Molly watched in silent terror as they gathered around the table, hastily unwrapping whoever it was they'd carried inside. It was hard to make out much of anything. Everyone was cloaked in black and soaking wet from the rain, moving at such a speed that they were just blurs.

But Rae should have guessed who it was from the look on Devon's face.

Her mouth opened in a noiseless scream as a hood fell away and Julian's head fell back onto the table. Pale as a sheet. Still as a corpse. And, like Devon said, he was very much—

"NOT BREATHING!" A mix of rain and tears flew off his face as he whipped around, staring helplessly at the men beside him. "DID YOU NOT HEAR ME?! DO SOMETHING!"

The next moments were some of the darkest in Rae's life.

They moved at a strange, stilted pace. Dragging along, then lurching forward so fast she could hardly see. Colors were too bright, sounds were too loud, and given the numbing shock that had clawed its way through her body, it would be a miracle if she remembered any of it the next morning.

At the same time, she knew it was a night she would never forget.

"Jules!" Devon sobbed, gripping the collar of his jacket. "I'm sorry! I'm so sorry!"

"Can't get it to stop bleeding," Tristan murmured, pressing down hard somewhere on Julian's ribs. "Do you know what blood type he is?"

"What does it matter?" Simon answered in a hushed undertone. "There's no time to get him to a hospital. We'll just have to work with what's here. Do you have any ice?"

"Yeah," Luke responded, backing away, white as a ghost. "I'll get it."

"Julian, please!" Devon begged, crying without shame. "Please open your eyes!"

"It doesn't matter if he bleeds out if he's already not breathing." Gabriel pushed past the two arguing men, and shoved Devon aside. *"Move."*

With shocking speed he leapt onto the table as well, pressing his palms together as he began to administer CPR. His lips moved silently as he counted out the beats, and every so often he would bend down to breathe into Julian's mouth.

Still, nothing happened. Equipped with her fiancé's tatù, both Rae and Devon could hear perfectly well that Julian's heart had stopped beating.

"*No!*" Devon sank to his knees, holding tight to his friend's arm as he hyperventilated into his other hand. Tears and blood were running freely down his face, but Rae didn't think that any of it was his. It all seemed to belong to Julian.

"Please," he whispered, pressing his forehead into Julian's wrist. "Please don't. Jules, you have to come back."

There was a slight pause in the rhythm, and Gabriel glanced down with dread. His eyes lifted slowly to Julian's face before he redoubled his efforts, upping his speed.

Tristan paled and backed away as Simon gritted his teeth and stepped forward.

"Do it harder," he commanded.

Gabriel never broke his stride. "Any harder and I break his ribs."

"Rae," Molly whispered, shrinking back, "I can't watch this. I can't watch him—"

"Your power!"

It was the first thing Rae had said since they burst inside, and for a split second the entire room turned to stare at her. She was shaking, head to toe. But her voice rang out against the walls.

"Gabriel, use your power. Keep his blood flowing!"

Gabriel froze in shock then stared down, wondering if it would work. The next second, he leapt off the table and took Julian's other hand. "Come on," he muttered under his breath, rigid with concentration, "work with me here."

At the same time Rae rushed forward, elbowing her way in between Simon and Tristan to get a better look at what was going on.

Big mistake.

The sight of it almost stopped her heart. Never before had she seen so much blood. So much destruction. If that much was on the table, how was it possible that Julian had any left?

"Okay," she put her hands on his jeans, trying to steady herself, "blood is just...blood. I should be able to conjure that."

"Are you crazy?" Luke gasped, having just returned with the ice. "There are specific proteins and antigens. Rae, what if you get the type wrong—"

"What's the alternative?!" she demanded. When no one answered her, she opened her palm and conjured a syringe and a tube. "That's what I thought."

With trembling hands, she rolled up Julian's sleeve and stuck the needle deep into one of his veins. As usual Alicia's healing tatù floated tentatively to the surface, but it was one of the more complicated sets of inks she'd ever received, and she'd yet to figure out how to use it. The only time she'd ever tried, ironically also on Julian, the psychic had strictly forbidden it. Implying that not only would she fail to help, but she would make things much, much worse.

"How are we doing, Gabriel?" she asked quietly. Half to distract herself, half because she was desperate to know.

He braced against the table, clenching his jaw with the strain. "There isn't much to work with."

A shudder ran through Rae's body, but she nodded firmly. "Well...that's what I aim to fix right now."

"You can do it," Devon breathed from the other side of the table. "I know you can."

Whether he was talking to her or to Julian, she would never know. But one thing was certain, they were both going to try...

Chapter 5

Rae had never focused so hard in her entire life. She swore nothing had ever been more serious. Never had the stakes been so high.

Her eyes closed as one hand clenched the open tube and the other drifted down to Julian's skin. It came up wet. Slick with blood. Exactly what she had intended. Tuning out everything else around her she rubbed her fingers together, slipping into one tatù, followed immediately by another.

First up was Ellie. If Rae wanted to conjure the right kind of blood, then she had to understand what it was she was working with. Fortunately, she knew a girl who was capable of doing exactly that. A hundred thoughts burst into her mind all at once. A hundred terms and sketches and calculations she could never hope to understand. Except, she *did* understand them.

And not a moment too soon.

Before she could lose focus she slipped immediately into Ethan's conjuring ink, letting all the knowledge she'd just acquired flow fresh through her veins and into Julian's.

There was a soft gasp beside her. Gabriel's green eyes shot open in wonder; he was staring down at the table with the faintest flicker of hope.

"It's working," he breathed. "I don't know if it's going to be in time...but it's working."

Rae nodded stiffly, every bit of focus locked onto her solitary task. "Once we get enough into his system, we need to restart his heart." Her eyes flashed across the room, coming to rest on her best friend. "Molly, you up for it?"

All the men in the room turned to stare as the tiny girl walked bravely forward. "Just tell me when."

Rae glanced questioningly at Gabriel, but he merely shook his head.

"I have no idea how much is enough, but I can't keep doing this much longer." Little beads of sweat were running down his face, mixing with the rain. "You can always give him more later."

Rae nodded solemnly and stepped away.

"Okay, Molls. Give it your best shot." Gabriel set his feet shoulder-width apart and braced himself.

The infamous Molly Skye needed no more invitation than that. With surprisingly steady fingers, she unbuttoned Julian's shirt and placed her hands on either side of his chest, pressing them gently into his bare skin. "I'm sorry," she murmured. "I know that I promised I'd never do this do you."

A swirling cloud of electric blue started building up behind her eyes—then came to a sudden pause. The entire table stared at her in breathless anticipation, but she turned to Devon instead.

"Dev," she said gently, "you have to let go now."

Rae's heart broke into a million pieces as she moved forward and took him by the wrist. No matter how urgent the circumstances, he seemed completely unable to let go of Julian's hand. After a split second, she had to literally pull the two apart. "He's going to wake up," she whispered, holding him tight. "He's going to be okay."

Devon's entire body held its breath as he leaned towards the table. "He has to be."

Molly flexed her fingers, then took a deep breath. "Okay. Here goes nothing..."

A bolt of electricity shot through her fingers, straight into Julian's chest. His body arched against the table, then fell lifeless once more.

Rae watched with bated breath, her heart hammering against her chest.

Little spiral of smoke began trailing up around them as Molly tried again and again. Then once more after that.

Every time he lifted, Rae's heart lifted, too. And every time he crashed back down, it broke into a thousand broken shards. Devon lived and died with each shock—flinching, like he was being whipped—as the tears continued to fall. The others merely stood and stared, growing more and more grim with each passing moment.

He's gone. I can't believe it. He's actually... gone. Rae brought her hands up to her mouth, watching in some kind of nightmarish daze. All the power in all the world, and she was going to watch her best friend die on the kitchen table. *How can this be happening? A few hours ago, we were all fine. Laughing by the fire...*

Molly was shaking now. Shaking so violently, it was hard to see that she was crying.

"You are not going to do this to me, Julian," she hissed through her teeth, building up a wave of power once more. "You're going to snap out of this, you're going to open your eyes and, damn it, YOU'RE GOING TO HELP ME RAISE THIS BABY!"

Another bolt shot through her hands around Jules' heart. Much stronger than the rest. His entire body lifted off the table before crashing back down.

Only, this time, something amazing happened.

This time...Julian opened his eyes.

"Jules?" Devon whispered.

No one dared move an inch as he blinked slowly at the ceiling, letting his eyes adjust to the bright light. It took a few seconds for him to realize where he was before he managed to focus on the tiny redhead hovering anxiously over his face.

"Jules...can you hear me?" Molly shouted loud enough to wake the neighborhood.

He coughed out a mouthful of smoke, then glanced down at his chest. Two little handprints were burned into his skin. Sizzling mementos of the worst hour of his life. "Molly Skye," he coughed out another cloud of smoke, "what have you done to me?"

A loud intake of breath filled the room as everyone remembered to breathe.

"Is this..." Devon took a halting step forward, pale as a sheet. "Are you really..." Words failed him as he returned to the table and took Julian's hand. His face tightened with an overwhelming wave of emotion, and a faint tremor shook through his voice. "We almost lost you."

Julian was still in a daze. "...lost me?" His eyes flickered curiously to Devon, lingering a moment on the bloody tear stains painted down his face, before looking around the rest of the room.

It looked like a bomb had gone off.

Rae stood clutching her heart with one hand as the other wiped away silent tears. No matter how long she looked at him, she couldn't believe it was true. That he was awake and breathing. That he had done the impossible and opened those beautiful eyes.

The second he spoke, Molly had half-collapsed on top of him. Her tiny arms circled around his waist as she wept openly into his bloody shirt, pausing every now and then to pick up his free hand and hold it against her cheek. Luke squeezed her gently but kept one hand on Julian at the same time, pressing the ice that was still in his hands absentmindedly against the psychic's ankle.

Even the adults were struggling to keep it together.

Simon closed his eyes in momentary relief, leaning shakily against the counter, while Tristan took what looked like his first breath since the lot of them had burst through the door.

Only Gabriel kept his composure. Granted, it was hanging on by a thread; Rae knew him well enough to see he was near the breaking point. "Julian?" He took a tentative step forward and stared apprehensively at the fallen psychic, like he was waiting for the other shoe to drop. "How're you feeling?"

It took a second for the question to register.

Julian glanced from the ice on his ankle, to the tube sticking out of his arm, down to where Molly was planting tearful kisses on his palm. For a second, it looked like he was more concerned for all of them. Then his face tightened with a sudden grimace.

"That's okay," Gabriel said quickly, nodding as though he'd been expecting it. "Jules, you got stabbed. Your body's in temporary shock, but we need to—"

"No...it's my hand." Julian gasped, and pulled weakly at his wrist. "You're breaking it."

Devon glanced down in surprise, then released Jules' hand with a look of horror. His pale skin lost even more color as he took a deliberate step away, utterly mortified over his mistake. "I'm sorry," he stammered. "I didn't realize—"

"It's okay," Julian replied gently, trying to get his bearings. "I just don't..." He trailed off as Gabriel's words registered, then looked down at his chest for the first time. "Wait...did you say stabbed?"

That's when the pain caught up with him.

A tortured cry escaped his lips, and the room snapped back into action.

Devon sprang back to the table, pressing a towel firmly against the open wound. Luke relocated the ice in an effort to slow some of the bleeding. Rae snatched up the tube and started conjuring, racing to get more blood into Julian's system than was streaming out onto the table.

I'm such an idiot! He woke up, but nothing's changed! Something still tore him open!

"Julian, stay with us, okay?" Gabriel circled around to the head of the table, placing his hands on either side of Julian's face and speaking with that practiced, reassuring tone he slipped into whenever things turned dire. "I want you to focus on keeping your eyes open. Can you do that?"

Julian trembled and nodded, but it wasn't entirely up to him.

"Where's your damn girlfriend, Gabriel?!" Devon demanded, switching out one towel for another as the first one soaked through. "Get her over here!"

"I told you," Gabriel muttered through his teeth, "she's not answering her phone. The Council was sending her as medical back-up into the field. She must have left already."

But Devon was too far gone to see reason. If Julian was going into shock, there was a good chance that his best friend would as well. "I don't care! Someone find out where she is and get her back here! We need—"

"No, we don't!" Molly interrupted quickly. Her hands were stained with blood from holding onto Julian, and there was a crimson smear across her cheek. "Rae, you have her power! Use it!"

An icy hand clamped down in Rae's chest, and she backed a step away. It was one thing to use Alicia's original diagnostic skill, but she had specifically avoided the healing aspect of her ability when they'd first come in for precisely the reason that she had no idea how to make it work. "I don't think I can," she whispered. Devon flashed her an indescribable look, and she shook her head quickly. "It's not a crisis of confidence—it's a fact. This isn't like conjuring! If I make a mistake trying to figure it out, I could..." she trailed off, unable to say the rest.

They had been down that road already. And far too recently.

Gabriel looked at her steadily before turning back to Julian.

His cries were softer now, his eyes less focused. That scary ashen tint had returned to his skin, and every time he pulled in a ragged breath a new wave of crimson splattered to the floor.

"Rae, I don't see that we have much of a choice," Gabriel said quietly. "You have to try."

"But, I—"

"There's no time!" Molly shrieked, shoving her forward. "It's the only option!"

How the freakin' heck is this coming down to me?! A wave of cold terror poured down her spine, but Rae jerked her head up and down and walked forward. Julian's eyes were drifting in and out of focus, and drifting in and out of time. For a split second she wondered if he was checking his own future, seeing if he made it through.

"Rae, you can do this," Gabriel said, his voice steady and confident.

"Okay." She rubbed her hands together, then held them over Julian's chest. "I can do this." *Except...I don't know how.*

"What..." Julian stirred weakly on the table. "What's going on...?"

"It's okay," Devon soothed, taking his hand once more. "Just stay with us, all right?"

"Guys," Rae whispered in a panic, staring helplessly at her hands, "how do I—"

"It's a force of will," Simon interjected encouragingly from behind her. "Tris and I had a healer back at Guilder. He used to say that he simply willed the body to knit itself back together."

Simple as that, huh?

With a look of the utmost concentration Rae took another step closer to the table, pressing her hands down onto Julian's chest. There was a painful hitch in his breathing and his eyes struggled to focus, but for once she was the one in a trance.

Will the body to knit itself back together...

Her eyes closed and she imagined it. Imagined the wound pulling itself shut. The veins beneath the skin repairing. The bones and muscles piecing themselves back together.

For a second, she thought it might be working. A strange heat started emanating from her hands as the ink blossomed up to the surface.

Then Julian started screaming.

Her eyes flew open as a host of other voices immediately joined in. Gabriel was telling her to keep going for a few seconds longer, watching as the wound began to close. Devon was shouting at her to stop, staring down in terror as his friend thrashed violently upon the table.

In the end, it wasn't up to her.

A hard shove caught her right in the chest and sent her flying backwards. Without Devon's tatù, she tumbled into the cabinets on the far wall before finally being able to catch her balance. A host of stars exploded before her eyes, but at that point it couldn't possibly have mattered any less.

Who'd pushed her? What—?

Julian lay propped up on his elbows, pointing a shaking finger at her chest as his dark eyes narrowed into a threatening glare.

Rae stared, her mind blank. Her mouth hung open.

"Hands off, Kerrigan. I told you to *never* practice that one on me."

Rae collapsed back against the cabinets in utter relief, sliding her face into her hands as a feeling of breathless exhaustion swept through her entire body. *He's angry! He has to be alive to be angry! And if he can shove like that, he's going to pull through!*

The next second, she and Molly descended upon him. Kissing, and hugging, and crying, and generally not letting him get any air until the boys eventually pulled them back.

"I'm sorry," Rae apologized, unable to contain the giant watery grin that had spread across her face. "I know you did, but I had to do something—"

"Let me die next time," he fumed, staring down painfully at his chest. She hadn't been at it long enough to actually heal him, far from it, but it had at least mended enough to where the immediate danger had past. "Honestly, I'd rate that right up there with you trying to conjure waffles."

The rest of the gang nodded seriously; they had been there for that catastrophe as well. But at the same time no one could seem to stop smiling. Joking and sarcasm were more of those 'signs of life,' and they couldn't have been more thrilled to hear them.

All except Devon, who still looked like he was recovering from a mild heart attack.

"You're...you're all right?" He sounded too afraid to hope. And too shaken up to possibly be thinking clearly. "You're really all right?"

No. Julian was clearly not all right. His skin was shock white, his eyes were bruised red, and torrents of blood were still leaking from the giant laceration in his chest.

But he seemed to sense the need to be. At least around Devon. "Yeah...I'm fine."

Devon didn't let his guard down for a second. Instead, he moved forward and took Julian's pulse. Then again. Then once more after that. Rae watched him closely but, to be honest, she didn't think he was even counting. She thought he was just making sure that Julian had one.

"Devon," Julian said softly, when it became clear there was no end in sight.

"Quiet. I need to count this out."

"But you've already done that—"

"Quiet, Julian. I'm counting."

Julian fell silent and bowed his head. A few steps behind him, Molly and Rae exchanged a quick look. As much as they might want to help, there was simply nothing to be done. Something had snapped inside, and only time would fix it. Time, proximity, and perhaps a small miracle.

"Dev..." Julian said gently, "I could have told you it would be okay."

Rae grinned. *I was right. He was checking the future. Checking to see if he was going to die.*

"But you couldn't." Devon pulled in an uneven gasp. Ever since carrying his best friend inside that night, he hadn't been able to breathe properly. "You weren't...you weren't moving."

There was heartbreaking tension in his voice, and the words resounded with every person in the room in spite of their best attempts to keep themselves together.

Molly and Rae exchanged a quick look, wondering what they would have done if it was the other. Simon shot a sideways glance at Tristan before staring down at the floor. Even Gabriel looked away with an imperceptible frown. Thinking of Rae? Thinking of Angel? They would never know.

Julian's face tightened before he visibly forced himself past it. "But I am now," he said quietly. "I'm fine."

The word *fine* wasn't going over well. Devon's eyes swept him up and down before he shook his head, an unspeakable expression on his face. "Then you can't possibly remember what happened."

All at once, a new kind of tension flooded the room. One that caught Rae completely off guard. It was a chilling reminder that she still had no idea what had happened. That she hadn't watched her best friend fight for his life at random. Someone had done this to him.

Before she could ask, Devon pressed Julian gently back onto the table.

"We've got to get that stitched up," he said softly. "You're still losing way too much blood."

Questions can wait. This can't.

Rae took an automatic step forward, as a vial of morphine shimmered into her palm. With any luck, Julian was in stable enough condition now that they could safely give him the shot without knowing the exact amount. To be honest, whether he was or not, she still might have tried. As someone who'd recently been stabbed, she knew all too well that the pain was excruciating.

Given that knowledge, she was shocked when he pulled away.

"No drugs," he murmured, taking a steadying breath, "I don't want to fall asleep."

Rae glanced at Devon, whose blank stare gave her no help.

Devon gave him a sympathetic smile. "Jules, trust me. You're going to want—"

"No." For whatever reason, his bloodshot eyes flickered up to Tristan and Simon before fixing with agonized determination on the ceiling. "Just stitch it up."

It was a fleeting gesture, but it caught the attention of everyone present.

What the hell is going on?!

Without a second thought, Molly stepped fiercely in between them, her hands crackling with lethal voltage. "It's all right, Jules," she said softly, speaking in a dangerous voice they rarely heard. "No one's going anywhere. Take the drugs."

He shook his head again and Gabriel stepped forward, taking the suturing kit Rae had just conjured out of her hand. "Don't force him. He's fine." He moved around Rae. "I've got it." With practiced hands, he grabbed a bottle of antiseptic off the counter and dumped about half of it onto a clean rag. The smell washed over the kitchen, and Julian's body stiffened with dread.

Even Gabriel flinched sympathetically as he pressed down over the wound, moving as quickly and efficiently as he could. A new river of blood poured over the alcohol, and Julian turned his head into the table with a quiet moan. "Sorry," Gabriel murmured, "I'm going as fast as I can." He dropped the towel the next instant, and picked up the suturing kit.

But the second the needle touched his skin, Julian paled dramatically and flinched away. "Devon," he gasped, "have Devon do it."

Gabriel pulled back at once. He and Devon shared a fleeting glance before the kit switched hands and one replaced the other. Whether it was the fact that only one had a speed tatù, or simply the fact that Julian had technically died that night and was searching for a security blanket, Rae would never know.

Devon knelt immediately and got to work.

It was gruesome just to watch. And Rae remembered all too well how it felt.

"Are you sure you don't want something?" Devon muttered, wincing apologetically as the needle dipped in and out. "Rae only skimmed the surface here."

Julian shook his head firmly, but his face was white as a sheet. Only a few seconds later, his eyes closed and his head rolled limply to the side.

Devon paused a second before pushing to his feet with a quiet sigh. Without looking away, he handed the kit back to Gabriel. "You're better at this than me."

Gabriel accepted it without a word, and moved to finish the job.

As counterintuitive as it sounded, it was somehow easier to breathe now that Julian was unconscious. Easier to form coherent thoughts when he wasn't gasping in pain.

Easy enough to ask one or two simple questions...

"Are you going to tell me what happened?" Rae asked quietly, aware that both Tristan and Simon hadn't moved a single muscle since Julian had shot them that look. "Or would you just like me to guess?"

It was hard to rein in her temper. Not as hard as it could have been, given that her shell-shocked fiancé was still trembling where he stood, but hard all the same.

Whatever had happened tonight, whatever the men had set out to do...she had been left behind. And *this*? Her eyes swept briefly over Julian's body. Maybe this could have been prevented.

But try as he might, Devon couldn't find it in himself to answer. All he could do was stare. "I made a huge mistake," he whispered, eyes locked on Julian. "A huge mistake."

It wasn't the answer Rae had been expecting. Molly, who had been eavesdropping from the other side of the table, shot her a similar look of confusion before they turned back to the men.

Gabriel had just finished bandaging Julian's ribs, and was pushing back to his feet. He alone didn't have the same sort of guilty comradery as the others. In fact, unless Rae was imagining it, he looked almost as angry with them as she was.

Of course, he was a lot more guarded with his emotions. "I'm going home," he said flatly, glancing around the kitchen without really looking at any one person. "I'll be back in the morning to see how he's doing. I'll keep calling Alicia, too."

Devon nodded quickly, grateful, but unable to put it into words.

Gabriel seemed to understand. He softened slightly, and even gave him a soft warning on the way out. "Don't tell Angel who did it. Not if you want them to live until morning."

Who did it?! Rae looked around the kitchen in horror. *One of them had—*

But before she could even think the door banged open, slamming against the wall as Gabriel was still reaching for the handle. His little sister stood framed in the doorway. Dripping wet. Shockingly pale. And looking like she could tear down London with her bare hands.

"Where is he?!" she demanded, fixing her cold stare on Gabriel. In times such as this, she only had eyes for her brother. "You just text me that he's alive, and to come home—"

"Because he is alive," Gabriel answered, suddenly sounding very tired. "It was a knife wound to the chest. He almost bled out, but we got him stable. He's sleeping now."

"Where?"

"In the kitchen."

Without another word she ripped off her wet coat and stormed inside, completely unconcerned with the fact that she was wearing nothing but combat boots and lingerie. A literal chill seemed to follow behind her as she swept straight past everyone else into the kitchen, only to come to a sudden halt in front of the one person she knew held at least some of the blame.

"Angel, don't freeze him."

The terrifying girl looked slowly at her brother before returning her gaze to Devon. Then she pulled back her fist, and punched him with such blinding speed Rae was sure she broke a bone.

Angel shrugged. "I didn't freeze him."

Without another word she vanished into the kitchen, forcing the current occupants to quietly relocate to some other room of the house. Gabriel glanced over his shoulder, hesitating in the doorway, but swept outside the moment Simon came into the room. Tristan, Molly, and Luke were quick to follow, leaving only Devon…Who was still bleeding where he stood.

Rae gave him a quick once-over before her lips thinned into a hard line. "Don't think you're getting off so easy with me." The two of them locked eyes, and she slowly shook her head. "You're not going to tell me what happened…you're going to show me."

Chapter 6

Julian was carried up the stairs. Flanked by Molly and Angel, and Devon was balancing him in such a way that his body was completely undisturbed. The second he'd passed out, Rae had given him a vial of morphine anyway. He was already asleep and whatever or *whoever* had made him hesitate, Angel wasn't letting anything get through that bedroom door.

The second she saw he was being settled in safely, Rae returned to the bottom of the stairs to wait for Devon's return. He had accepted her terms of interrogation without a fight—as radical as they might be—but she already had a pretty good idea as to what she might see.

"Hey, do you mind if Molly and I stay here tonight?"

Rae turned around to see Luke standing behind her, his arms piled high with an assortment of blankets and pillows. Everything from the downstairs bedroom.

"Of course, but what—"

"They're for Molly," he said with a little sigh. "Not only is she not speaking to me, but she's setting up guard in the hallway outside Julian's room. Unless Angel lets her actually sleep inside."

I highly doubt it. And given the look on Angel's face, I highly doubt Molly even asked.

"Of course you can stay, Luke," Rae muttered, her eyes still fixed on the landing. "You know that the two of you never have to ask."

He did know that. But it had seemed a good icebreaker for what he wanted to say next. "Rae, I..." his blue eyes tightened, and they dropped down to the floor. "I'm really sorry about all of this.

I didn't want to go in the first place, but then when your—" He stopped suddenly short, staring just over Rae's shoulder.

She whirled around to see her father and Tristan walk out of the darkness. Standing tall, side by side.

"Goodnight," Luke muttered, disappearing before they had the chance to speak.

Rae watched as he hastened up the stairs before turning slowly to the men standing behind her. One had the audacity to meet her gaze, while the other still looked utterly demoralized.

"I'm going to sleep in the car," Tristan murmured. "I want to be here first thing in the morning when Julian wakes up." He held out a hand towards Simon. "Give me the keys."

Simon dropped them into his palm without taking his eyes off his daughter, and the man disappeared without a word. It was only then that Rae saw Julian wasn't the only one who got hurt that night. The scarf wrapped around Simon's hand was stained with blood.

"I don't suppose you'd like to tell me what happened," she said through gritted teeth.

Simon's eyes tightened sympathetically as Devon appeared at the top of the stairs, took a second to steady himself, then began trudging slowly down to the foyer. "I suspect you're about to get that answer right now."

Rae turned with a glare to find herself face to face with her fiancé. Devon looked as exhausted as she had ever seen him. The deep bruises beneath his eyes gave him a haunted glow, and his cheek was still bleeding steadily from where Angel had punched him.

His eyes flickered only once to Simon before focusing entirely on Rae. "I got a..." The words caught in his throat, and he shook his head. "*I* decided to go after Samantha."

Rae raised her eyebrows but said nothing. She had suspected as much. She just wasn't sure where the rest of them fit in, and what had gone so terribly wrong.

But Simon wasn't willing to let Devon take all the blame alone. "I texted you," he said with a soft frown.

"It was my call." There wasn't a hint of doubt in Devon's voice, and a dark shiver shook through his entire body as his eyes flickered to the trail of blood leading up the stairs. "I did this."

Rae held up a hand. Demanding to hear them both out. Unwilling to do it together. "Go upstairs," she commanded softly. "I'll be up in a minute, and we'll...*talk*."

Devon hung his head, and obeyed without a word. Slipping automatically into his tatù, he blurred up the steps so fast neither Rae nor Simon could follow until they heard the door shut.

The second it had, Rae turned back to her father. "Let me guess. You were the one who texted him earlier tonight. Told him to meet you some place in the dead of night. Convinced him to go on this suicide mission with you." Why had she not thought of this sooner?

Simon gazed at her steadily, denying nothing. That sort of thing wasn't really in his nature. "It didn't take much convincing."

No. After what she'd told Devon just a few hours earlier, she didn't imagine it did.

Unable to tell her father how terribly perfect his timing had been, preying upon the fears of a new father—she diverted to the smaller issues instead.

"How the hell did you even get his number, Da—Simon? How do you even have a phone?" She remembered what Tristan had said, and raised her voice. "How the hell do you have a car?!"

And WHERE is my MOTHER in all this?

Simon absorbed each question silently, staring back with that unshakable calm. "I think the question you really want to ask me is, why I didn't text *you*."

Rae's blood rose to a boil, and she fought to control her temper. She had been in enough interrogations and played enough passive-aggressive games not to rise to the question.

Instead, she merely folded her arms across her chest and looked her father right in the eye. "Wrong again, Kerrigan. My only question is this: would it have been worth Julian's life?"

The quiet words did more than any amount of screaming ever could. Simon's mask of calm shattered, and she could see the unspeakable guilt welling up beneath. The gut-wrenching misery that plagued his every breath.

Good. No one deserves it more.

Without another word, Rae turned on her heel and headed up the stairs. She wasn't going to interrogate her father. She wouldn't believe a word he told her anyway. Besides, there was someone waiting upstairs who required her immediate attention.

"You can stay the night, or go back to Kent," she called over her shoulder. "I really couldn't care less. But you'd better not be here in the morning."

She heard the front door slam shut as she slipped silently into her room.

Devon was sitting in the center of the bed. Although the walls were already beginning to turn pink with the coming sunrise, the promise of a bright new day, he looked completely spent. His perpetually bright eyes were dull with stress and fatigue, and locked on her with something close to dread.

"We promised each other that we'd never have any secrets," she murmured as she sank beside him onto the bed. "That we'd never sneak off or lie...that we'd do everything *together*."

They had whispered the words to one another shortly after Devon proposed. In one of the last quiet moments before the tatùed army in Scotland had marched upon Cromfield. They had seemed so simple at the time. So easy to commit to, Rae never thought they'd be sitting here now.

"I know." Devon let out a shaky sigh and bowed his head. His entire body seemed to wilt with remorse. "Rae, I never planned to—"

"Give me your hands."

A sudden silence fell between them as they stared into each other's eyes. The weight and horror of the night crashed down upon them, and for a moment nobody moved. Then, without breaking her gaze, Devon silently extended his hands.

They were cold. Cold and smeared with dried blood.

She took them without hesitation, squeezing them automatically, before remembering herself and turning them over in her own. Carter had told her once that his gift was easiest to use when the subject was fatigued. When the mind's usual defenses were broken.

But Devon wasn't just another subject. And she had never trespassed into his mind before.

"Close your eyes," she whispered. She didn't want him looking at her. Didn't want him watching as she stole inside. "Try to relax. I'm only looking at one thing."

One thing. They both knew it wasn't true. Carter's ink didn't work like that. Once you were inside a person's mind, anything was up for grabs. Their entire life—past, present, and future—was an open book. Every thought. Every dream. Every memory and feeling. All of them, exposed.

Devon nodded, then grew very still. Waiting.

So, get on with it, Kerrigan. Rae's hands tightened with anticipation as the ink rose to the surface of her skin. But the moment it had, she found herself just as frozen as Devon. Completely incapable of the next step.

"I can't." She dropped her hands and drew back onto the mattress, bringing her knees up to her chest and shuddering at what she'd almost done. "I can't do it."

His words would be enough. Enough to make her understand. Enough to show her any critical information she might have missed. They simply had to be.

"Just tell me what..." But her voice trailed off as Devon picked up her hands once again.

"Use the ink," he said softly. Her eyes widened, but he stared back with a faint smile. "I have nothing to hide from you. We've already agreed to share our lives together. What's mine is yours." His fingers laced through hers, bringing them automatically to his lips for a kiss. Then, before she could say a word, he closed his eyes and bowed his head, bracing for what was coming.

Rae stared for a second before pulling in a deep breath and doing the same. *I love you. So much. Maybe too much.* She swallowed, needing to find the answers. *Here goes nothing...*

The ink hit them like a tidal wave, fusing their hands together as a quiet gasp escaped from their lips. Then, as quickly as it hit, they froze in perfect unison.

This is it... Rae looked around in wonder. *This is the man I'm going to marry...*

It was truly incredible. Like nothing she'd ever seen before.

The first thing she noticed was the light. Everywhere—bright light. It was as if his entire mind was awash with it. Illuminating every thought. Setting every memory aglow.

While most people pulled her down, spiraling into the depths of their thoughts, all of Devon's were right up on the surface. Just waiting for the slightest glance or touch to send them spilling out into existence.

Because he wants to do this. Because he's waiting for me.

A feeling of love and completion washed through her. So intense that it would have lifted her off her feet had she been standing. The stronger it became the more the world around her brightened in response, as if he sensed her feelings and reflected them back in his own. The connection between their hands warmed with a tender glow, and had Rae's eyes been open she was sure she would have been smiling.

But she hadn't come here to explore the beautiful wonders of Devon's mind. She had come for a specific purpose, to see a specific thing. A thing that had no light at all.

As if on cue, the world around her dimmed. She rotated, staring with wide eyes as the picture slowly changed. It got dark and wet. Then waited...inviting her to step inside.

The second she did, everything changed.

"What the—?!"

It was like getting sucked into a black hole. Yanked off her feet, spinning, flying, only to come crashing down into the real world. Harsh reality slapping her upside the brain.

That's more like what I was expecting.

She opened her eyes, and all at once she was right there. Standing inside a moment from just a few hours before. Before the world had fallen apart. Seeing it all through Devon's eyes.

The way he lay silently beside her, waiting for her to fall asleep. The way he kissed her softly on the forehead, and whispered a silent apology, before stealing away into the night.

Rae ghosted along beside him as he crept into the room at the end of the hall, where his friends slept soundly on the bed. Not taking any chances, he clapped a hand over Julian's mouth and tilted his head towards the window. Julian glanced at Angel in surprise, then followed without hesitation. He dressed quickly, and they leapt out the second-story window with effortless grace.

Julian's face lightened with surprise when he saw Luke waiting for them on the wet pavement, then lightened again as Devon started walking not to his car, but down the street.

"What's going on?" he asked quietly, once they were a safe distance away from the darkened house. "Where are we going?"

Devon stiffened. "You'll see."

A few blocks up, they ducked into a bar. One that Rae must have walked past a million times, but had never really noticed until that moment. They wove their way through the noisy crowd, ignoring the drunken people around them, to a table in the very back.

"What the hell's going on?" Julian stopped dead in his tracks. "What is *he* doing here?"

Rae whirled around and almost shouted the same question herself.

Moving like the villain in some cheesy horror film, Simon Kerrigan slowly leaned out of the shadows, folding his hands upon the table. Tristan was sitting beside him, staring at an untouched drink. He glanced up as well, although he looked about as eager to be there as Julian.

"Lower your voice, kid." Simon gave him a teasing wink. "We don't want to make a scene."

A scene?!

In a blur of shocking speed, Julian leapt over the entire table and punched Simon in the face.

Punch was a bit of a generous word. *Punch* implied something you could come back from. If Simon hadn't been gifted with certain supernatural talents, there was a good chance that *punch* could have killed him on the spot.

"Julian!" Luke pulled him back down to the floor, looking just as stunned as Simon. They had no idea about the file. About the damage it had caused. "What the hell's the matter with you?!"

Julian said nothing. He simply stared at Simon with the darkest expression Rae had ever seen on his handsome face. One that promised terrible things to come.

Tristan glanced in astonishment between them, while Devon's face tightened with a look of profound remorse. But Simon was starting to look like he understood. His eyes softened the longer he stared across the table, then thawed completely as he bowed his head with a sigh.

"He knows." Julian spat on the sidewalk.

"Knows what?" Luke demanded, still holding Julian back. "Julian, what the—"

"He has every right," Simon interrupted quietly, picking up a napkin to wipe at the blood dripping down his face. "He has every right."

"Shut up, guys. It's a conversation for another night." Devon stepped between them, trying to steer the unlikely group back on task. "I wouldn't have asked you here if it wasn't important. Simon texted me earlier tonight. Apparently, he...he has some information."

Luke looked at Devon curiously, while Tristan cast a sideways glance at Simon, obviously wondering where exactly this crucial information had come from.

Julian, however, took one final look at the table before he turned on his heel and walked away.

"Jules," Devon rushed after him, catching him by the sleeve, "please...for me."

Rae watched silently as he and Julian shared a long look. It was moments like these when she'd swear they were telepathic. The psychic's dark eyes hardened, but when it came to Devon there was very little he would refuse. After a tense moment he nodded curtly, and the two of them returned to the table.

"So, what is this information?" Luke demanded. He may not have known what precisely had his friends so upset, but he didn't need another reason to hate Simon Kerrigan. "Spit it out."

Simon's eyes flashed as a sinister smile ghosted across his face. "I know where Samantha is."

There was a moment of silence as everyone present absorbed it as best they could.

Luke was simply surprised, while Devon's eyes flickered nervously around the group. Julian was unmoved, but Tristan was staring at his son with a curious expression, looking almost pleased.

"That's why you called me?" Tristan asked in surprise. "To help you with Samantha?"

Devon froze guiltily for a second, looking suddenly unsure of the answer himself. "You can walk away," he said quickly. "You don't have to—"

"No," Tristan downed his drink with a sudden smile, "we'll take her out together."

Luke's eyebrows lifted slowly as the point of the meeting became abruptly clear. While the three men were obviously on the right track, there seemed to be some vital people missing from their group. Julian saw it at the same time, and gave Devon a hard stare.

"You're asking me to go with *him*?" Julian asked quietly. "You're asking me to do this?"

Devon looked like he was being torn in two. One half was truly horrified to put his friend in such a position, the other half was begging him to see it through. "I'm asking you to protect Angel from what's coming. I'm asking you to help me protect Rae—" His voice broke upon saying the name, and his eyes shone with true panic. "Julian, you know why I can't...why I can't just..." He bowed his head with a fractured breath. "Jules...*please*."

Rae's eyes welled up with tears, and she lifted a shaking hand to her mouth. No one else but Luke knew what they were talking about, but the question Devon was really asking was clear as day.

Please help me protect my unborn child. Please help me eliminate this threat.

As godfather to my child...please fight for it.

They locked eyes for what felt like an eternity before Julian sighed imperceptibly and glanced away, looking suddenly tired. "All right."

The rest of the memory became nothing more than a blur.

Simon had apparently picked up a tracking tatù. Rae assumed it was the same ink that belonged to the man Beth had hired to keep tabs on him. And Simon had found Samantha's flat there in the city. It was less than a twenty-minute drive, and she had no reason to believe they'd be coming.

It would be easy, he said. It would be quick.

The men piled into a car waiting outside. A car Rae assumed Simon had also somehow taken from his keeper. They shot away into the city, weaving their way through the darkened streets before coming to a sudden stop about three blocks away from a run-down apartment complex.

No one had said a word in the car, and no one talked now. They simply stood in an ominous-looking huddle on the sidewalk—their breath frosting into clouds as they gazed up the street.

Finally, Devon cast a sideways glance at Simon. "Are you sure she's inside?"

Simon nodded, a look of hungry anticipation sharpening his face. "Fourth floor. Second door on the right." He cocked his head suddenly to the side as his lips turned up with a sudden smile. "She's asleep. Or at least, she's in the bedroom."

A faint shadow clouded Devon's eyes before he looked down with a quick nod.

The idea of killing an unarmed sixteen-year-old girl as she slept might have been unsettling, but he also had plenty of images of the same such girl trying to murder his future wife. The mother of his child. The one effectively cancelled the other.

"Okay," he said softly, slipping into the same decisive tone Rae remembered so well from their missions together. "I'll go in first with Jules. The rest of you provide cover. No one gets too close. With any luck, we should back outside in less than a minute." He pulled a gun Rae had never seen before out of his jacket, and screwed on a silencer. "...And then this whole thing will be done."

No one disputed the plan. In fact, no one said another word as they crept inside the building and made their way up to the fourth floor. The lights flickered on and off above them as they ghosted down the hall, coming to a stop at the second door on the right.

Without a word, Luke sank to his knees and pulled something silver out of his pocket. Any of the men gathered, including him, could have kicked it down in a second, but they needed to be quiet. They needed the girl not to wake. He fiddled around with the lock for a second before it swung open with a low creak, casting an ominous glow of moonlight into the darkened hall.

Devon and Julian exchanged a quick look, and stepped inside together. The other three were just a few steps behind. Rae found herself literally holding her breath as they silently made their way across the living room, their eyes locked on the door at the end of the hall.

It pushed open without a sound, and for a second all was still.

Samantha was there all right. Sleeping, just like Simon had guessed. It if was possible, she looked even younger than Rae remembered. Her dark hair spilled out over her pillow, and every so often she would shiver with the chill, clutching the blankets tighter around her chin.

A strange look passed over Devon's face as he lifted the gun. Preparing to cross a line, after which he would never be the same. His eyes closed for the briefest of moments as he placed a finger on the trigger. Praying for forgiveness? Praying for strength? Then he pulled in a deep breath.

...and all hell broke loose.

As Devon's finger squeezed upon the trigger, he was tackled suddenly from behind. The bullet lodged itself in the wall a few inches away from Samantha's pillow as Simon knocked him down and raced towards the bed. A chorus of shouting suddenly echoed in the quiet room, followed by one piercing scream as Samantha sat bolt upright and stared in terror at the scene in front of her.

Simon was tearing towards her with his hand open, a hungry gleam in his eye.

He wants her tatù, Rae realized with a chill. *It was always about her tatù. That's why he came.*

Julian made a wild grab for him, but missed. Luke grabbed for the gun, but it had flown from Devon's hand. Tristan grabbed his son by the shoulders and pulled him out of harm's way.

Leaving nothing in the world between Simon Kerrigan and his greatest prize...

...except Gabriel.

He came out of nowhere, flying past them like he'd been given wings. A split second before the tips of Simon's fingers could touch Samantha's skin he leapt into the air and tackled the man with all his strength, sending them both somersaulting across the floor.

They hit the wall with a deafening thud, and for a second nobody moved.

...then all hell broke loose again.

A feral scream shook through the air as Samantha leapt to her feet. She might have looked like a peaceful child when she was sleeping, but awake she was a tigress. Ready for the kill. "You...I can't believe you just..." Her eyes came to rest on the gun before widening to a terrifying size. "Every single one of you will pay for this," she muttered. "You have my word."

The next second, she was gone. Not fled. Not escaped. Just...gone. Like she'd simply vanished into thin air.

Rae whirled around, desperately searching, but it was like trying to find a ghost. For all they knew, Samantha had commanded them not to see her. Commanded herself to appear invisible as she slipped out onto the fire escape or into the hall.

At any rate, the mission was a complete failure. But the night was just getting started.

"What the hell was that?!" Luke shouted, scrambling to pick up the gun. He quickly reloaded it and whirled around in every direction, but the girl was gone. "Simon, what did you do?!"

On the other side of the room, Simon and Gabriel were still picking themselves up off the floor. There was a human-sized dent in the plaster where they'd slammed into the wall, but Gabriel seemed to have gotten the worst of it.

He blinked heavily as a stream of blood slipped down from his golden curls. Then looked up in a daze to see Simon towering over him with a terrifying expression on his face.

Nothing happens to him, Rae told herself reassuringly. *You're going to see him just a few hours from now. He's fine.*

However, looking at her father's face, she couldn't be so sure. He looked about a second away from ripping Gabriel in half, but in the meantime there was something he wanted even more.

That same hungry expression flashed across his face, but before he could take a single step forward Gabriel's hand shot up between them.

"Give me a reason," he said softly. A crimson stain dripped down the side of his face, but he looked up at Simon with steady, lethal eyes. "Give me a reason and I'll do it."

Simon stopped where he stood. Looking at the hand. Looking back at Gabriel.

The rest of the room was still in an uproar. No one noticed the quiet exchange between the two men. Each of them was lost in his own panic. Trying desperately to regain control.

"She couldn't have gotten far!" Luke's hand was still clenched around the gun, pointing it alternatingly between the door and the window. "Devon, can you hear her?"

Devon shook his head, closing his eyes with concentration as he tried. A few feet away, Julian was having similar luck as he tried to see down a million paths of what might happen.

If only they had been paying attention. If only they had noticed the way Tristan's eyes had glazed over. The way he stepped purposely away from the rest.

I can't see this! A wave of panic shook Rae to the core as she stood helplessly on the sidelines—watching the nightmare unfold. *I can't just see it happen!*

Julian was standing in a trance, staring off into the future. But for the first time, it looked like he didn't quite believe what he saw. A faint line creased down the center of his forehead as his lips parted in surprise. He was still coming out of it when the knife sliced through the air.

Rae let out a silent scream that no one could hear.

It happened too fast for anyone to stop it. Too fast for anyone to see. The blade slipped in and out of his chest. Eliciting only a quiet gasp and a fleeting look as he fell noiselessly to the floor.

The scream that followed was much louder, but it didn't come from Julian.

"JULES!" Devon dove beside him, trying to catch him before he hit the floor. But for once, he wasn't fast enough. His movements were palsied with shock, clumsy with fear. He was so thoroughly beside himself, he didn't even see what was coming until it was too late.

"Devon—" Julian gasped. His face was drawn with fear and pain, and his eyes were locked on something just over his friend's shoulder. "Dev, behind—"

Devon turned just as the blade flew towards him. Stained red with the blood of his best friend. Held firm in the hand of his father.

There was nothing he could do. It was too fast. He was too stunned. He would only watch with wide eyes as it flashed through the air. Leaving him with time only to whisper a single word. "...Dad?"

It should have been the end. It was a lethal blow, one that no one could survive.

But somehow, it wasn't.

A hand flashed into the air between them. Absorbing the blade meant for another. Impaling almost in half as the knife stabbed straight through the center, coming out on the other side.

There was a feral cry of pain as Simon Kerrigan leapt onto the scene.

"Tristan—NO!"

In what had to be the most selflessly excruciating tactic Rae had ever seen, her father actually twisted Triston's hand in a perverse wave, using his own flesh and blood to rip the knife away. It flew away from Tristan and landed with a loud clatter on the other side of the room.

There was a small scuffle as Simon launched himself forward, pinning his best friend up against the wall. But Tristan didn't fight him. The second the knife dropped, the trance broke with it. Leaving the rest of the room reeling in the aftermath.

Luke was shaking, while Gabriel had gone very still.

Devon was still looking at his father. Frozen with almost childlike shock. It wasn't until something wet soaked through the knee of his jeans that he looked down to see Julian bleeding out on the floor beside him. "Jules!" he cried again, forgetting everything else entirely as he lifted his head off the floor. A look of sudden dread paled his face as he pressed down on his friend's chest, only to have his hands immediately overrun with blood. When he spoke again, it was far less sure. "...Julian?"

Gabriel jerked in place, like someone had snapped their fingers beside his ear, then bolted across the room in a flash, sinking to the floor beside them. "We have to get him out of here," he muttered, trying to assess the damage as best he could between the torrents of blood and Devon's trembling hands. "Help me lift him. On three." He counted down swiftly, but when the moment came Devon didn't move.

Not everyone had been raised in the catacombs. Not everyone had learned to suppress all human emotion. Devon's best friend in the world was dying on the floor of a cheap apartment.

...a part of him was dying, too.

"Julian, stay with me." All his training and experience went right out the window as he ripped off his jacket and pressed it against the wound. His voice shook, and his hands were trembling so violently they could hardly hold on. "It's going to be okay. It...it *has* to be okay."

It was a heartbreaking scene. One that made even Gabriel pause.

On the other side of the room, Tristan peeled himself off the wall. He blinked slowly as he returned to the present. Looking like a man who was coming out of a nightmare, only to realize that it wasn't a nightmare after all.

His eyes flickered first to his son, sweeping Devon up and down in a practiced way to make sure he was safe, before coming to rest on the blade still embedded in Simon's hand. "...Simon?"

At once, Simon dropped what he was doing and rushed back to Tristan's side. It was like the last fifteen years never happened. Like they were brothers once more.

"What...what happened?" Tristan breathed, stepping back as he reached to Simon for support. "I don't..." He trailed off when he saw Julian, his face growing dangerously pale. "Simon, please tell me...please tell me I didn't do that."

The two shared a look of silent understanding and Tristan slumped back against the wall, looking like he was going to be sick. On the other side of the room, things weren't much better.

A sea of tears blurred Devon's eyes as Julian began to drift in and out of consciousness.

"I don't know what to do," he whispered, staring down at his blood-stained hands. "You're the one who can see the future. Please...tell me what to do."

The words were for Julian, but the psychic was fading fast. It was Gabriel who answered.

"We take him back to the house."

"The house?" Luke echoed, almost as lost as Devon. "But the hospital—"

"The house is closer," Gabriel insisted, pulling him up to a sitting position. His green eyes tightened as Julian's arms fell limply to his sides, and he muttered under his breath, "He's not going to make it to the hospital."

The words carried farther than he intended, and for a second the entire room froze.

It was a testament to how bad things were that they hadn't moved him already. That everyone was still standing in the dingy little room. But it only took one look at Julian to see that his situation was critical. No one wanted to risk moving him. They were afraid just to touch him.

"*Devon.*"

Devon looked up sharply as Gabriel jerked his head towards the door.

"Are you going to take him? Or am I?"

The words brought the room back to life.

Luke nodded and ran downstairs to bring around the car, while the younger men bundled Julian as best they could for the journey. As for the older generation, they kept their distance.

There wasn't a single drop of blood for which they weren't directly responsible. No matter how the situation might have changed, it was a fact that was impossible to forget.

And the rest was history.

Julian let out a soft cry of pain as they carried him down the stairs, but other than that he remained quiet. Quickly slipping into the near-comatose state that would claim them by the time they reached the house. The others never spoke a single word. Not until they rounded the corner to the London house, and Devon shouted the fateful words.

"HE'S NOT BREATHING!"

The memory faded to mist as Devon and Rae lifted their heads at the same time. The deep violets and midnight silvers of the garish scene brightened into the soft light of morning. The warm glow of the rising dawn had crept inside the room.

Although the mental connection was broken, they didn't let go of each other's hands. And it took a moment to realize they both had tears in their eyes.

"Now you know." Devon bowed his head, overwhelmed by the images all over again. "Now you know everything. Rae, you have to believe me; I never meant to—

"*Shh.*" She put a finger over his lips, and pulled a blanket over them in the same instant. She didn't want to talk about what happened. It was enough to see it. It was enough to see what it had done.

"Hold me," she whispered, pulling his arms around her with a little shiver. "Please just hold me."

Chapter 7

Rae woke a few hours later to a set of the most vile profanities she'd ever heard. At first, she thought some sort of Irish sailing convention must've come to town before she realized the dark litany was coming from her best friend's room at the end of the hall.

"Devon," she whispered excitedly, turning to shake him although there was no way he could possibly have slept through it. "Devon, it sounds like Julian's—"

But Devon was already gone. The sheets cold. The bed on his side was empty.

Instead of the automatic dread that usually followed such a discovery, Rae found herself grinning uncontrollably as she leapt off the mattress and grabbed the first set of clothes her hands touched. She dressed quickly, racing down the hall. The door was half-open, and from the sounds of things she wasn't the only person who was completely beside themselves at the prospect of seeing Julian alive. In fact, unless she was mistaken, the colorful commentary wasn't even coming from him.

"Get the hell *OFF*, Molly!"

There was a muffled struggle, followed by a dull impact, followed by the sound of breaking glass. Immediately after, a burst of electricity lit up the entire second story.

What the...?! Rae skidded to a sudden stop, staring wide-eyed at the door. The tips of her raven-colored locks reached up to the walls as an invisible wave of static electricity rippled through the air.

"MOLLY ELIZABETH SKYE!"

Devon's voice shook the house—the thunder behind the lightning—as Rae ventured a few steps closer. The door to Julian and Angel's bedroom wasn't ajar, as she had originally thought. It was actually propped up precariously in the frame, a giant scorch mark running up the center. A rarely used tatù floated to the surface of her skin, and with a mischievous grin she vanished into thin air before slipping silently into the room to watch the strange scene unfold.

It was exactly as she might have predicted.

Molly and Devon were standing at the foot of Julian's bed, screaming at each other like it was the end of the world. The room around them was in shambles. Burnt curtains. Shattered desk. A thick layer of smoke hung in the air, and every now and then a shower of angry sparks would fly off Molly's fists, adding fuel to the fire.

As for poor Julian himself? The subject of all their indignant rage?

He was lying unnoticed on the mattress. Propped up in the center of the bed on a trio of blood-stained pillows. His face was pale and tired and, judging by his expression, he had been watching them go at it for quite some time.

High-strung. Rae shook her head with a little grin. Over the years, she'd heard her friends rather generously described as high-strung. *Yeah, I can see it...*

"I can't believe it!" Devon cried, running a hand along the back of his head as a fine layer of singed hair fell to the ground. "I can't believe you used your tatù on me!"

As if to accentuate his rage, a broken picture frame fell off the wall.

"It's not like you left me a choice," Molly hissed, clinging onto the foot of the bed like her life depended on it. "Trying to BAN me from the room! Are you bloody SERIOUS?!"

"BECAUSE YOU'RE TOO LOUD!" Devon shouted at the top of his lungs, completely oblivious to the ridiculous irony echoing off the walls. "Can't you see you're upsetting him?!"

Julian sighed softly and slipped lower on the bed.

The others were too distracted to notice.

"I'M upsetting him?!" Molly's face paled with fury. "I'M not the one who took him out last night and almost got him KILLED!"

Devon ducked swiftly as she pelted him with her shoes. "This is EXACTLY what I mean! Lower your DAMN voice!"

Julian's dark eyes flickered wearily between them, growing more tired with each pass. When a bolt of lightning followed the stilettos, he tried to gently intervene. "Guys—"

"Don't try to talk, Jules," Devon quieted him quickly, blurring to the side of the bed. "You'll only strain yourself."

"But I'm really—"

"Seriously, Julian." Molly took up position on his other side, distractedly smoothing, then re-smoothing his dark hair. "What you need right now is peace and quiet."

He closed his mouth helplessly, and the two of them proceeded to continue to scream at each other.

"You need to be careful with him!" Devon shot Molly a scorching glare as he seized Julian's wrist to check his vitals. "It's like you're not even paying attention!"

"I'm plenty careful with him, thank you very much!" Molly wrapped her tiny arms around Julian's neck defiantly, patting the top of his head. "He needs me right where I am."

Neither noticed the ironic wince that tightened Julian's face every time he was touched. Nor the silent sigh that bowed his shoulders. In the end he simply settled back on the bed, watching his friends with a look of long-suffering patience as they went for each other's throats.

It wasn't until Rae shimmered into view that he glanced up with a spark of hope. Their gazes locked for a suspended moment, his lovely eyes screaming a silent cry for help.

Get me the bloody heck out of here.

Rae lifted her hand with a little salute, and stepped boldly into the fray. "Ahem!" she cleared her throat loudly, and the other two jumped in surprise. It wasn't often she was able to catch them both off guard, and she took a second to revel in the triumph. "From what I can see, the biggest threats to Julian's well-being right now...are the two of you."

Molly and Devon froze at the same time, flushing guiltily as they looked first at Julian and then down at the floor. Both mumbled an unintelligible apology and took a step back. The psychic flashed Rae a look of extreme gratitude, which she specifically avoided—preparing for her betrayal.

"Now," she clapped her hands briskly together, taking advantage of their silence to seize her golden opportunity, "I think the person Julian really needs to spend some time with is *me*—"

Julian's head fell back against the pillow as the shouting started once more.

"Not on your life!" Devon countered, enraged once more. "He needs to rest! I'm not going to stand here and keep arguing with—"

"If Rae gets to stay then I get to stay, too!" Molly screeched, clinging even tighter to Julian's neck. "I'm the one who cares about him most—"

Rae shot her a sarcastic glance, sending a gust of wind to mess up her hair, and Devon literally picked her up in frustration, trying to pry her away.

"Are you kidding me?!" Devon scoffed. "How are you *possibly* the one who—"

"I'm his ROCK!" Molly's legs were lifted into the air, but her arms held firm. "You have no idea half the things the two of us have..." She trailed off suddenly as a chilling silence fell over the room.

The three friends took a giant step back as a breathtaking girl took a giant step forward, her sapphire eyes flashing pure murder.

"What the hell is this?"

Oh, crap. Not good.

The three friends stepped back farther still and Julian collapsed against the pillows with a sigh of relief, running his hands up over his face with a muttered, "Oh, thank goodness."

"Did you think this was what I meant when I said to keep an eye on him?" Angel's voice rang with a deadly sort of calm. The kind that left everyone looking for the exits. "Really?"

Rae fought the urgent need to once again become invisible as Molly angled discreetly behind her. Only Devon had the strength to answer, although he couldn't seem to meet her eyes.

"We were...we were just—"

"GET OUT!"

Rae didn't argue. The terrified feeling inside her, the urge for flight instead of fight, won out. She skittered out of the room like her feet were on fire, the others hot on her heels. She turned around at the door to watch Angel, wanting to make sure Julian was okay. She didn't say a word; neither did her fiancé or best friend.

Julian, however, gazed up at his girlfriend with a tender smile. "What do you have there?" he asked softly, nodding at the bag still clutched in her hands.

She turned back to him, her fearsome expression melting back to exquisite perfection. "I brought you some breakfast..."

Devon did them the courtesy of discreetly propping the door in its hinges on his way out and, together, the three friends headed down the stairs, feeling rather subdued, all things considered. "So, uh..." he raked a hand awkwardly through his hair, "anybody hungry?"

Rae nodded at the floor, while Molly piped up, "I could eat."

He nodded once, not really looking at either of them, and disappeared into the kitchen.

The second he was gone, the girls shared a silent look.

"I wasn't scared," Molly said defensively.

Rae glanced back at the top story with a shudder. "Me neither. Not for a second."

Luke joined them for breakfast, and an hour or so after they'd finished eating the front door pushed open.

"Hello?" Dean Wardell called quietly as he stepped inside. "Anybody awake?"

The four friends stiffened of one accord. They were settled in the living room, surrounded by a dozen cups of coffee. Luke had already filled Molly in on what had happened, and now that they were satisfied their friend was in good—albeit terrifying—hands, they were quietly discussing what to do about the other catastrophe that had happened the previous night.

That catastrophe being Samantha.

"Anybody here?"

Devon glanced up to where Julian was resting upstairs before getting to his feet. "I'll tell him to leave. I'm sorry, I didn't even think he might still—"

Much to his surprise, Rae stopped him. She held onto his sleeve, glancing at the others for affirmation, before gently shaking her head. "Dev, it wasn't his fault," she said softly, lowering her voice as much as possible, even though Tristan would still be able to hear. "Julian knows that. You need to know it, too."

Devon froze for a second before pulling his arm away. "I don't care," he muttered. "I can't see him in here. I can't...I can't see him at all."

A wave of pity welled up inside her as she remembered the look on his face. That almost childlike look of wide-eyed shock as his own father bore down on him with a knife.

But she remembered the look on Tristan's face as well. After the trance had broken and he realized what he'd done, she felt certain he was about ready to turn that knife on himself.

"You can't blame him for something that wasn't in his control." Her dark hair fell around her face as she bowed her head with a little sigh. "Devon...I didn't blame you."

That stopped him.

His eyes tightened, and for a split second they both flashed back to just a few weeks earlier. When Devon had been the one with the blade. The memory was enough to make him sick. A look of gut-wrenching sadness swept across his face, and he sank silently into his chair.

"We're in here," Rae called, keeping her voice as steady as she could. The sound of light footfalls echoed in the foyer, and a second later Tristan Wardell swept into the living room.

It was clear the poor man hadn't slept a wink. Rae doubted he'd even made it to the car. His eyes flickered quickly across the living room—resting for a painful moment on his son—before he turned and glanced up the stairs the same way Devon had just seconds before. Rae felt sorry for him.

"Is he all right?" His voice wavered, as if he could hardly say the words out loud. A scary sort of tension had stretched him to the brink, and Rae didn't want to imagine what might happen if he didn't get the answer he needed. "Did he...did he make it through the night?"

"Of course he did," a deep voice answered. Rae looked up with a start as her father walked up behind Tristan, clapping him on the back. "He was through the worst of it when we left him."

Flames of ice-blue fire shot from the palms of Rae's hands as she leapt to her feet, pointing a smoking finger at her father. "What are you doing here?! I told you not to come back!"

He held her gaze as Devon quickly stood up behind her, placing a steadying hand on her back. She felt his cool breath on her neck as he murmured into her ear.

"Rae...Simon saved me."

The words were soft, yet effective. Just as she had reminded him a moment earlier.

Rae glanced around the room. Molly's hard look had softened. Luke glanced up with a begrudging glare. Devon was prepared to let the man back into the house. Only she remained immune to the 'noble' sacrifice.

"He saved you *after* putting you in danger in the first place," she spat. "That's what he does." Her heart had literally stopped the moment her father had taken the knife intended for her fiancé, but that didn't change why there were there in the first place.

"Rae," Luke reasoned quietly, "we all decided to go—"

"And then my father decided to change the plan." The fire spread up her arms, forcing Devon to take a step back. "Samantha would have been gone by now—a bullet to the brain—if my father hadn't decided to try to steal her tatù instead. The threat would be over! She'd be dead!"

But that, it seemed, was the other half of the problem.

Devon stiffened, staring down at his hands as if he could still see the gun, before a silent sigh escaped his lips. "Rae...he saved me from doing that, too."

She turned back to him at once. The fire vanished as tears filled her eyes. She'd never considered the possibility. Never imagined that, in some small way, he was relieved. Grateful.

In a way, it made sense.

Devon would not be the same man if he'd pulled the trigger. No matter how hard he could have justified it, or what rationalization he tried to make—he would always have been slightly broken by it. Slightly less. On top of that, the man had saved his life. Rae had seen the look on his face when Simon threw himself between him and his father. Taking the blade into his own hand. Standing between Devon and certain death.

But when it came to Simon Kerrigan, intention was everything. It was a lesson that Rae was only beginning to understand. One that she'd been warned of from the very start.

"He didn't do it for you," she murmured as she sank back into her seat. "He did it for the tatù. For the power. He doesn't care about any of you. Or me. He wants our abilities." Her eyes lifted with a searing glare. "He tried to take Gabriel's as well."

The others whipped back around in shock. They had been too distracted by the sky falling around them to see what had happened on the other side of the room. Even Tristan glanced beside him, his eyes searching Simon's for the truth.

But Simon only had eyes for his daughter. "I wouldn't have taken Gabriel's power. Not without his permission."

A cold, cruel laugh echoed in the room. One that Rae was surprised to discover had come from her. "Liar." She held her gaze against his. "You want his power. And you know he'll never give his permission."

He'd tried to take it before. Ever since Gabriel was five years old, her father had coveted the extraordinary ability running through his veins. He'd done everything imaginable to steal it.

Their eyes held for another moment, and a faint shadow flickered across Simon's face. She knew the story. There wasn't a doubt in his mind that she knew.

If only it would make a difference...

"This isn't about Gabriel's tatù," Devon said softly. "My *life*, Rae. He saved my life."

Her eyes flashed as she stared into his. "And we almost lost Julian's."

As if on cue, there was a soft shuffling at the second-story landing. The entire room held its breath and watched as Julian limped stiffly down the stairs. One hand was clenched around the banister, while the other held tightly onto Angel. His face was set hard against the pain, but there was a look of unmistakable pride shining just beneath the surface.

"Jules, what are you doing?" Devon leapt immediately to his feet to help—racing halfway up the stairs to take his other hand. "It's way too soon for you to be back on your feet."

"I was bored," Julian flashed him a tight grin, "and I figured you guys were probably all down here pining for me." He had yet to notice the two surprise guests in the room, focusing instead on the task at hand. "Actually, I had a vision that I can't manage the last step." He gestured briskly ahead. "Could you—"

"Yeah." Devon gently half lifted him and set him carefully back on his feet, his face tightening in concern at the faint smear of blood that had appeared on the side of his friend's shirt. Julian, on the other hand, couldn't have been prouder. He glanced back at the staircase like it was his own personal Everest before lifting his eyes with a genuine smile.

...then he froze.

"Julian."

Dean Wardell had turned into a statue the second he saw Julian coming, his face going shock white as he stared up with some uncertain emotion. Even now he didn't seem to know whether to step forward, or keep a careful distance. His every decision would be based on what Julian did next.

Julian...tripped.

It was hard to tell if he'd tried to continue forward, or if he'd jerked automatically back towards the stairs. Either way, it was a painful mistake. He gasped quietly as Devon caught him, and leaned all the way back into his best friend's and Angel's steadying arms.

"Dean Wardell," he said faintly. Strange how those adolescent titles refused to fade. "I'm sorry, I...I didn't know you'd be here."

Typical of Julian to apologize to the man who'd plunged a knife into his chest.

A look of quiet devastation tore across Tristan's face as he took a tentative step forward.

"I can leave," he offered swiftly. "I don't have to—"

"No, no, of course not." Julian tightened his grip on Angel. Half to restrain her, half for support. "I was just...coming down to see what we were going to do about Samantha."

Another typical Julian move. Shifting attention away from himself.

"*We* aren't going to do anything," Angel said firmly, leading him to a sofa on the far side of the room. "You're going to rest. It looks like you already pulled one of your stitches." She fussed over him for a second, flashing a lethal glare. "You did just get *stabbed* after all."

Tristan turned a delicate shade of green before sinking into a chair. Simon stared another second at Angel, and settled down beside the dean.

How old was she the first time he saw her? Rae glanced between them with sudden, morbid curiosity. *She couldn't have been more than just a toddler. A baby maybe?* The thought twisted inside her. *Like her baby?*

"Whatever we do about Samantha, it's going to have to be quick." Luke unwrapped his arm from Molly's shoulders and leaned forward onto his knees. "She knows we're after her. And the last thing she did before vanishing into thin air was swear her eternal revenge. We need to move fast."

Devon nodded swiftly, turning to Simon. "Where is she now?"

Simon met his eyes for a split second, his brow furrowed with a frown. "Excuse me?"

"The tracking tatù," Devon replied. "The one you used to find her in the first place. Where does it say we need to go?"

A look of sudden understanding flashed across Simon's face. Followed by sudden fear. "The tracking tatù. Of course." He shifted uneasily in his chair, looking hyper-aware of the fact that

Devon's father was sitting beside him. "I don't...I don't have it anymore."

"You don't have it?" Devon repeated blankly. "But you can't just lose an ink, can you? I thought it had to be replaced with another—"

"I took yours."

Tristan made a compulsive movement, while Devon's face lightened in honest surprise.

"Mine?" He glanced reflexively down at his tatù, as if checking to see whether it had been diminished somehow. "That's not possible. When would you have even—"

"When I knocked you to the ground," Simon replied quietly. "I knew you wouldn't feel it."

A deafening silence rang through the room as each person processed the information. Some were angry, some were afraid, others were simply shocked.

After a few moments Simon felt Tristan's eyes burning into him, and chanced a nervous glance at his friend. "It's a good thing I did. Otherwise I might not have gotten there in time—"

"*After*," Tristan interrupted quietly. He met Simon's eyes, suddenly looking very sad. "That all happened *after* you stole his tatù."

"It amounts to the same thing."

"It *means* something completely different."

Rae folded her arms tightly across her chest, staring at her father like she'd never seen him clearly until that very moment. He didn't care about Devon. Or, if he did, it was simply as an afterthought. He needed the fox ink for speed. He needed to be fast enough to get Samantha's tatù.

Gabriel was right about him. Gabriel's been right all along.

But then a quiet voice spoke up from the corner. Saying the last words from the last person that anyone expected to hear.

"You saved Devon's life."

The room went dead quiet as they turned to look at Julian. He was propped up painfully in his chair, staring at Simon with a curious expression dancing in his dark eyes.

"Last night," he spoke in a soft undertone, working it out as he went along, "I remember you...you saved him." The two men locked eyes for a long moment, then Julian inclined his head. "...Thank you."

Just two simple words, but they ended the question of Simon's inclusion once and for all. As furious as everyone was, as astonished as everyone was, if Julian could forgive the man—who were they to judge?

"Come on," Angel said quietly, helping him to his feet. "We need to change that bandage."

The crimson stain on his shirt had now spread to the other side and Julian followed along without protest, giving Tristan an inadvertently wide berth as they headed to the kitchen. The others watched them go before turning back towards the center. Feeling strangely numb.

"So...where does that leave us?" Molly asked quietly.

Rae leaned back in her chair with a tired sigh. "It leaves us right back where we started."

Chapter 8

Rae got up early the next morning, even before Devon. She slipped into his tatù for absolute silence as she dressed quickly and headed down the stairs. The rest of the house was still fast asleep. Julian had overdone it slightly with the stairs, and had spent the better portion of the afternoon paying the price. As no one in the house was willing to leave him alone for even a second of the grisly recovery, it had been a long day for all of them.

Unwilling to use the noisy coffee maker Rae conjured a steaming shot of espresso in her hands, followed immediately by two more. She threw them back in quick succession, then pulled on her boots and headed out the door.

The air was crisp and grey, charged with that anticipatory stillness that usually happened right before it began to rain. She glanced up nervously before breaking into a little jog. The park that separated the gang's various London homes was beautiful, and on any other morning she would have taken her time. Promise of rain or not.

But this morning was different. This morning, there was someone she needed to see.

"Hey, Capri," she greeted the receptionist behind the front desk as she sailed into Gabriel's apartment complex. "Looks like it's going to rain."

To call the building where Gabriel lived an apartment complex was a ridiculous understatement, and to call Capri a receptionist was laughable at best.

The place looked like it had been constructed as some whimsical pastime by the same guy who did The Louvre and Westminster Abbey. Just two buildings down from Molly and

Luke's penthouse, it had the same ritzy-modern feel, while maintaining a strong sense of 'old-world' beauty as well. Tall stone pillars stretched up into the sky, inlaid with intricate carvings depicting paintings and people long since passed. The lobby itself was fitted with a breathtaking mosaic of stained glass, and if it wasn't for the steaming cappuccino maker in the corner Rae might have guessed that she was in a museum.

The entire place was manned by a woman who looked like she'd stepped straight out of a Renaissance portrait and into a designer mini skirt. Capri Romano was hands-down one of the most beautiful, intimidating people Rae had ever seen, which was saying a lot in the tatù world. Standing at an impressive six feet, she would have looked more at place on a catwalk than answering phones behind a desk.

Unfortunately, the only person she was interested in seemed to be the only person immune to her seductive charms.

"Been raining all week," she answered without looking up from her nails. Capri was friendly enough to most people, but was decidedly less so to girls who visited Gabriel's apartment. She'd clearly fallen madly in love with him the day he'd moved in, and the fact that he had yet to even notice her was a source of increasing frustration. "Want me to call him?"

"No, it's all right." Rae flashed her a quick smile as she breezed past. "I'll just head up." *One day, she's going to stab that nail file into my back...*

Avoiding the elevator in favor of the stairs, she bounded up to the second story and flew down the hall to Gabriel's flat. After shattering his door on her last visit—an unfortunate canine feat of strength—he had found it prudent to make her a key. She searched around in her purse for a moment before jamming the thing into the lock and storming inside.

"Gabriel?" she called, making a quick rotation in the living room. "You awake? Shoot, you even here?"

The place was sparse, but tasteful. And incredibly neat. After spending the better part of his adolescence beneath ground, Gabriel had developed a strong aversion to all things unclean.

"*Gabriel!*"

A sudden wave of citrus steam poured into the room as the bathroom door opened and Gabriel walked into the living room—naked, save for the small towel wrapped around his waist.

For a second, all Rae could do was stare. She might be desperately in love with the man she was about to marry, but that didn't mean that she was immune to the man in front of her. She still had eyes, after all, and Gabriel wasn't really the kind of guy you could ignore.

Clouds of steam rose off his muscular shoulders as his golden hair fell damp around his neck. Little rivers of water found their way into the sculpted grooves of his bronze skin, trailing down his chest and stomach in a way that sent a blushing shiver across Rae's skin.

"You okay?" he asked, concern etched in his eyes but hidden everywhere else.

A blossom of heat reddened her cheeks as she mentally slapped herself senseless. He was staring at her with a faint smile, his head tilted to the side to get her attention. Was he concerned because she'd just barged into his apartment, or because she wouldn't stop staring at him?

Freakin' wake up, Rae!

"Uh...hey," she stammered, averting her eyes. "Sorry, I guess I should've called. I didn't realize how early it was."

He shrugged, grabbing a water bottle off the counter and taking a quick swig. "I just got back from a run. What's up?"

A damn good question. One that she'd been asking herself a lot lately.

"I just...wanted to get out of that house for a while." She dropped her eyes to the floor, more troubled than even she had realized. She looked up slowly. "Do you have a minute to talk?"

He cocked his head towards the bedroom, and she followed along. That citrus smell was almost overwhelming—in an intoxicating way—and she found herself absentmindedly wondering if she should open a window. The bed was made and she perched delicately on the edge, watching as Gabriel rooted around in his closet before twirling his fingers teasingly in the air.

She grinned and turned around. The Gabriel she knew didn't give a crap if she saw him naked. In fact, he probably would've welcomed it. But ever since he and her fiancé had battled it out a few weeks ago in Kent, he'd made a concerted effort to rein the impulses back.

Not that he was always successful.

"All right. I'm...decent."

She turned back around with a mischievous smile. "I guarantee that no one, in your entire life, has ever described you that way."

The towel had been replaced with a pair of faded jeans, and he was digging around in his dresser for a shirt. A little grin tugged at the corner of his lips as he grabbed one. "You wouldn't be wrong." He lifted the shirt to his head, then paused suddenly. "Would you prefer that I didn't? It looked like you were enjoying yourself."

He wouldn't be wrong... "Would you stop?" She smacked him with a pillow she tossed and he pulled the shirt over his head, shaking out his wet golden waves with a quiet chuckle. "Why do you keep doing that?"

He settled beside her on the bed, unapologetic as ever. "Why do you keep showing up at my apartment?"

She flashed him a rueful grin. "Because we're *friends*, Gabriel. And I need a *friend*."

He smiled and leaned back on the pillows, stretching his arms above his head. "I can be a friend." He made it seem like the easiest thing in the world. "I can be as friendly as you want me to be. Just say the word."

She laughed quietly, tracing invisible shapes into his blanket. It felt good to laugh. After the last few days, it felt good to even smile. But the longer she sat there, the harder it was to do.

"Hey." Gabriel dropped his playful banter at once, leaning forward instead with a look of concern. "What is it? What's going on?"

Rae stared down at the blanket, feeling suddenly cold. "They forgave him. My father." The edges of her world seemed to darken as a sharp breath caught in her chest. "Since he saved Devon's life...they all forgave him."

Gabriel said not a word. He looked neither surprised nor upset. He put his arm around her shoulders, but said nothing to soothe Rae.

"It's so obvious," Rae ranted on, well aware that she was preaching to the original choir. "It's *so obvious* that he's just manipulating the situation. But it's like...it's like they can't see it."

All evidence to the contrary, Gabriel acted the gentleman. He didn't harken back to the time when he'd said those exact words himself. He didn't show even a shred of frustration. He simply nodded once, lifting his eyes with a look of unending patience. "They won't be able to," he said without judgement or blame. When Rae looked at him questioningly, he shook his head. "It's a powerful thing...when someone saves your life. It's a debt you can't shake easily. No matter how hard you try." His voice trailed off near the end as his eyes lifted to stare vacantly out the window.

Rae's heart tightened as she realized they were thinking about two different people. She was thinking about her father. He was thinking about Carter. "He really cared about you, you know," she said quietly. "He always did."

Gabriel looked back with a start, staring her up and down like he was worried she'd started to lose her grip. "Rae, your father *hates* me. Why would you possibly—"

"Carter," she said quickly, flashing him a grim smile. "I meant Carter."

The word hit like a battering ram, freezing them both. For a second, Gabriel dropped his arm off her shoulder and simply stared at her, looking as though he would have given anything in that moment to be anywhere else, then he bowed his head with a quiet, "Oh."

A suffocating silence overtook them once more.

They hadn't talked about Carter since that day at the factory. As far as Rae knew, Gabriel hadn't talked about it with anyone. The second they'd gotten back on English soil, he'd locked himself away. Barricading himself in his apartment so long, she was afraid he'd never come out.

She couldn't blame him. Gabriel's life had changed forever that day. The moment Carter leapt in front of him, taking the lethal bullet into himself. It had changed in ways he couldn't begin to imagine. In ways he didn't want to imagine.

"Don't be too hard on them, Rae." He finally managed to break the silence, looking up at her with a tight smile. "They want to see the best in people. That's a good thing. It's not something you ever want to change."

"But you knew," she insisted, staring hard into his eyes, "you knew all along. You know what he is, that he hasn't reformed. You tried to warn us—"

"People don't change," he said simply. "They are what they are. To hope for something different...Rae, it will only hurt you. Every time."

A profound sadness swept through her from head to toe, flooding into every bit of open space in her body. It was a heartbreaking perspective to have, and yet he meant it. Those words that might sound so foreign or scripted to others had kept him alive.

She stared at him, wishing she could erase all the pain and hurt inside of him. "You changed."

Gabriel looked up in surprise, his emerald eyes sweeping over her before hardening with a humorless laugh. "Yeah. That would make things easier, wouldn't it?"

It was cold and rhetorical, but she couldn't help but respond. The Gabriel Alden she knew now was entirely different from the man who'd broken her out of jail. The one who wouldn't let down his guard for anything. The one who'd hid his murderous plans behind a charming smile.

That Gabriel had wanted to take her life. This Gabriel would do anything to save it.

"You have, Gabriel. It's not just me. We all see it." Her breath caught in her chest for a moment before she reached out to take his hand. "Carter saw it, too."

A look of unspeakable sorrow tightened his handsome face, dimming the very light in his eyes, before Rae realized he was going to deliberately shift the conversation in another direction. Gabriel didn't do well with conversations of the heart, or any seriousness that didn't involve trying to kill someone.

"What's the plan with Samantha? What're we going to do?"

Rae leaned back against the headboard with a sigh, stretching out her legs as she gazed up at the ceiling. "I honestly don't know. We'll have to wait and see."

"She'll be back."

"I know." Rae pressed her lips together tightly.

They contemplated this for a while. Sitting in a troubled silence. Staring out the window.

Finally, when it could go on no longer, Rae turned to him with a little smile. "The last time I was here, I was a wolf."

Gabriel glanced back at her with a grin, drops of water still clinging to the tips of his lashes. "You ate my duvet."

For the next two weeks, the house by the park fell into a strange sort of rhythm. One where everyone kept their heads down and played their part, even though no one knew how much longer that could possibly last. Travel was limited, unofficial curfews were established, and visibility was kept to a minimum as, together, they waited for that last proverbial straw to break.

Alicia was nowhere to be found. After a few more days of watching Julian suffer, Rae had gotten on the phone and called up the acting mission commander for the Privy Council. It was like Gabriel had said. She had been sent deep undercover to keep watch on a trio of agents, and wouldn't be back for the next few weeks.

Meaning that Julian was having a *long* recovery.

Rae felt horrible. She couldn't remember the last time one of them had been forced to wait it out and heal just like a normal person. By the end of the first week, he was drafting up comical versions of a will. By the end of the second week, he was ready to search the globe for Alicia himself.

But there were positive steps as well. On only the fourth or fifth day, he and Tristan had buried the hatchet. It was a memory which still brought tears of laughter to Rae's eyes.

Devon's father had come by early in the morning, the same thing he'd done every day since he'd unintentionally buried a knife in his son's best friend. He'd breezed through the door to find Devon, Rae, and Molly settled on a blanket in the backyard, watching with great amusement as their beloved Julian finally succumbed to the wonders and delights of conjured narcotics.

"I just don't understand," Julian was saying, gesticulating with grand motions he didn't seem to notice himself, "what if you happened to be accidentally leaning against the platform? You weren't expecting anything extraordinary, you were just leaning. Would you melt through then?"

Rae shook her head as Molly leaned forward with a serious frown.

"No, you wouldn't. It not like you can trip into the wall and accidentally find yourself on the path to wizarding greatness. It has to be intentional."

The others talked about these things in the hypothetical. Molly did not.

Julian nodded, his eyes as wide as saucers.

"Well what about the phone booth, then? The one that gets you down into the Ministry of Magic? What if you were walking past and simply happened to place a call?"

Devon shot Rae an exasperated grin as their friends began discussing it at great length.

"Why did you have to show him those movies?" Devon muttered, leaning over to whisper in her ear. "There was a reason I kept them from him. He's going to obsess for weeks."

"You can't *stifle* his magic, Devon." Rae removed his arm from her shoulder, turning back to Julian with a theatrical smile. "All he has to do is believe."

The magic was slightly lost on her fiancé.

"Well, I've been to King's Cross Station," Devon replied with a smirk, "many times. Trust me, Jules, there's nothing inherently fantastical about that place."

"Maybe you just weren't looking," Julian mused, staring off into the distance as a whole world of possibilities opened before him. "You could have stumbled upon something amazing..."

Devon clapped him on the shoulder with a grin. "I could have stumbled upon hepatitis."

A throat cleared softly and they turned around to see Tristan hovering in the doorway, wearing a faint smile. One foot was inside, and one was out, as if he wasn't sure where he'd be allowed. "I can see I'm interrupting something important..."

Molly stood up with a grin, dusting off her pants as she headed inside to make them all a pitcher of lemonade. "Julian had never seen Harry Potter. Thinks he's missed his calling."

"Ah, I see." Tristan flashed her an indulgent grin before settling down on the patio furniture. Close enough to be part of the conversation, but far enough away so as not to cause any alarm. "This a part of your recovery, then?"

"A critical part," Julian answered, his eyes growing heavy as his head fell absentmindedly upon Rae's shoulder. It had been his longest day so far out of bed, and the drugs were beginning to get on top of him. "Actually, we should watch the rest of them, just to be..." He trailed off, running his fingers through her dark hair with a look of pure wonder. "Rae, your hair is *really* soft."

Devon's eyes twinkled as Rae kissed the back of his hand with an affectionate smile. "Why, thank you. And we'll watch all the movies. Whatever you want."

As if to second his enthusiasm, Annie-the-puppy, who had joined them in the yard, promptly reappeared. Wagging her tail with fierce pride, she presented Devon a mouthful of flowers she'd painstakingly uprooted from the garden.

He took them with a beaming smile. *"Good girl!"*

It never failed to crack Rae up. The special voice he'd developed just to communicate with their dog. He praised and cooed, ruffling her golden fur as she puffed out her little chest with pride.

"Look who found the flowers again!"

Julian looked on with a detached sort of amusement. "It's a good thing we bought this place," he said to himself. "Otherwise we'd never get the freakin' huge security deposit back."

Rae grinned, gently helping him to his feet. "I think that boat pretty much sailed the first time Molly used her tatù in the house."

"You watch your tongue!" Devon scolded with a wink, holding the dog against his chest with an adorable smile. "Annie's on a mission just like the rest of us."

Julian and Rae exchanged a quick look, but between the puppy and narcotics they could think of not a single suitable response. Instead, they simply waved and limped towards the house, giving Tristan a parting nod as they passed him by.

But, as it turned out, Tristan hadn't come to see his son. He'd come to see Julian. He leapt to his feet as Rae reached for the door, and quickly steadied the psychic's other arm.

"Julian, I was hoping you might have a minute." He stood politely to the side, his face friendly and nervous at the same time.

Julian's lovely eyes latched on him with a curious stare, glassed over from the two vials of morphine Rae had given him before breakfast. "Did you want to watch the movies, too?"

Tristan stifled a grin and shook his head, taking a step back to see him better. But the more he did, the more that grin faded from his face. Replaced with something serious. Something sad. "Julian, I'm so sorry."

His tone abruptly shifted the mood of the happy little yard, and Julian stiffened as the shield of narcotics lifted momentarily from his mind. "It's all right," he said softly.

Tristan's face tightened painfully, and he reached out without thinking and squeezed the psychic's shoulder. No matter how distant he and Devon might have been over the last few years, the man had watched the two boys grow up. Julian was like a second son. "No, it isn't. Of course it isn't," he murmured, shaking his head. "Julian, I can't even begin to tell you how—"

"It's okay; you weren't yourself." The words were quiet, but sincere. It looked like Julian had honestly dismissed it. Forgiven it without thought. While he was still bleeding.

Tristan's face tightened again, and he looked him up and down. "That's unbelievably generous," he said softly, "but you don't have to—"

"We don't get mad at people for that around here."

The words rang out in the sunny little yard, resonating with every person inside. Even Molly stopped in the doorway, clutching the lemonade as her face softened into a thoughtful frown.

It was true. How many times had Samantha's power been turned against them? How many times had they done things they could never take back? Things they could never hope to repair?

The only answer was forgiveness. Blind, extraordinary forgiveness.

Julian had that in spades.

Plus, he was still a little high.

"Besides," he continued conversationally, "I always figured you kind of wanted to. Ever since I accidentally backed your car into the pond over that Christmas break."

There was a sudden silence. Followed by a tentative smile.

"That was you?" Tristan's face lightened in amused disbelief as his son paled and discreetly angled behind the puppy. "I always thought it was Devon."

Julian shook his head, oblivious to the desperate looks his best friend was giving him from across the yard. "No, it was me. We figured Devon should take the fall because you wouldn't expel your own son. Or kill him."

Ironically, both assumptions hit a little too close to home, but Julian was too disoriented to realize it. He simply leaned into Rae with a sleepy smile, tangling his fingers distractedly in her hair.

Tristan pursed his lips with a bemused smile. "And you figured now was the right moment to tell me?"

Julian nodded, wide-eyed and solemn. "It seemed like an appropriate time."

Rae quickly steered him back into the house before either one of them could hear the repercussions of that little confession. Switching into a strength tatù, she helped guide him slowly up the stairs, before laying him down gently on his bed.

"Angel?"

"She's still at Gabriel's."

"Good." He closed his eyes a moment. "I'm glad she has him for a brother."

"Me, too." Rae watched him a moment. "You ready for some more?" she asked, conjuring a vial.

He glanced at it then shook his head, closing his eyes once again. "Nah, I'm spinning already." Instead, he simply opened his arms, a silent invitation.

Without a second thought Rae kicked off her shoes and nestled into him, curling his strong arms around herself with a contented smile. They lay there in a comfortable silence for what seemed like a small eternity. Relaxed in each other's company. Safe, if only for a fleeting moment.

"It's weird, huh?" he murmured, letting out a peaceful sigh.

She glanced up curiously, studying his handsome face. "What is?"

He opened his eyes, and looked down at her with a fleeting smile. "Did you ever think when we met at Guilder that we'd end up here? That our lives would be like this?"

She hesitated a moment, snuggling deeper into his arms, lost in thought. "No. I don't think anyone could have predicted this."

There was a beat of silence, followed by a silent laugh that shook Julian's chest slightly. "Well...it *sucks*."

She glanced up again before joining in, too, keeping her weight carefully off his chest as the two of them fell to pieces. For a moment, the surreal absurdity of their situation washed away every other emotion, and they laughed until they could laugh no more.

When they finally quieted down, the silence hit hard. Just as hard as the sudden laughter. The two of them froze for a moment, thinking again, before he gave her a swift kiss on the forehead.

"One way or another, there's no one I'd rather be here with than all of you."

She squeezed his arm as unexpected tears blurred her eyes. "Live for the moment, right?"

He laughed again, shifting painfully as his chest began to bleed. "Yeah...live for the moment."

Chapter 9

Live for the moment, right?

The next morning Rae knocked on the door of her best friend's apartment, prepared to say the words that Molly Skye had been waiting her entire life to hear. Two coffees were clutched in her hands, and her foot tapped nervously against the floor as she waited in the hall. Wondering, for the millionth time, why she didn't already have a key. There was a faint shuffling on the other side, followed by an irritated, *"I'll get it—I'm only pregnant,"* before it swung open, revealing a petite redhead dressed in a Gucci bathrobe and a pair of Donald Duck slippers. The bathrobe had been a gift from Rae. The slippers from Luke.

For a moment both girls simply stood there, staring at each other.

"Rae?" Molly asked curiously, glancing up and down the hallway to see if anyone had come with her. "What are you doing up so early? It's not even—"

"Will you help me pick out a wedding dress?"

It was like the heavens had opened. Like that fateful gong had finally been rung.

Molly's jaw dropped all the way to the floor as her eyes simultaneously widened to take up at least half of her face. A strange gasping sound tore its way out of her body and she started trembling head to toe, rattling the enormous curlers still pinned in her hair.

"Are you kidding?" She snatched up her purse and joined Rae out in the hall, her eyes flashing electric fire. "Let's do this."

Rae burst out laughing. "One sec there, Molls." She made her best friend go back inside long enough to remove the curlers from her hair and throw on some clothes. Luke was unceremoniously woken and sent away to 'play with the boys' before the two girls clinked their coffees together and headed off down the street.

It should have come as no surprise that Molly just happened to know the exact street address of every bridal boutique in London, but Rae still couldn't help but be impressed when she unzipped a side compartment in her purse and pulled out a ready-made map.

"Okay. So, we can start at Phillipa Lepley, then head over to Brown. London Bridal is in the same part of town. Or if you want, we can just head straight to Vera Wang."

Rae grabbed the map, staring at the color-coded routes dotted with little x's along the way. "Molls, when did you even make this thing?" She turned it over with an incredulous frown to skim the index on the back. "It looks like some of it was done in crayon."

"In the third grade," Molly answered promptly. "A boy named Marco Marconi asked me to marry him by the swings and I got planning the very next day. Can never hurt to be too prepared."

"...too prepared?" Rae unfolded the bottom crease to discover a glossary of terms.

"For your *wedding*!" A hand shot out and Rae looked up in surprise to see Molly beaming back at her, a million happy tears sparkling in her sky-blue eyes. "Rae, you're getting *married*!"

A girlish grin swept up the sides of Rae's face. The caffeine was kicking in, and Molly's enthusiasm was catching. Before she knew what was happening the two of them were jumping up and down on the street, shrieking with high-pitched squeals before darting off down the street.

The first boutique they went to didn't take people without an appointment. The second boutique said the same thing, and Molly 'accidentally' set a plant on fire on the way out.

But the third boutique...that one showed a lot of promise.

"Oh, Molls..." Rae clasped her hands together, gazing in wonder down the endless rows of breathtaking gowns. Shimmering pearl satins, sleek ivory silks, tufts of alabaster tulle. Just standing in the middle of it made her feel like she had wandered onto some heavenly cloud. That kind that came with accessories and little flutes of Champagne. "This is perfect."

"Isn't it, though?" Molly sighed, staring around with that same dreamy expression. The kind that came from watching two decades of romantic comedies. "It makes you almost sad that, in theory, we're only supposed to wear it once."

A radiant smile danced across Rae's face as she lifted her fingers to brush the edge of a veil. "That's not necessarily true. You could always pull an Elizabeth Taylor. Break up with Luke every couple of years, just so the two of you can get married all over again."

Molly put down the tiara she'd been modelling, and whirled around with instant approval. "Rae Kerrigan, that's probably the smartest thing you've ever said." Her eyes lit up with a new realm of possibilities as she gazed further into the store. "It's certainly the most practical..."

"Well hello, ladies!" An eager looking saleswoman glided towards them on heels that had to be at least twelve inches tall. "Good morning!"

"Morning!" Molly and Rae chanted back in unison.

The woman looked them up and down, pursing her crimson lips in a playful frown. "So, who's the lucky lady? Which one of you are we shopping for today?"

Molly took a step away from the display table, and wrapped her arm around Rae's waist.

"My friend here just got engaged—"

"Both of us," Rae interrupted. She ignored the woman's look of surprise, and wrapped her own arm firmly around Molly's shoulders. "We're actually both getting married."

The woman nodded swiftly and wrote something down on her clipboard as Molly shot Rae a sideways look from the corner of her eye. Her forehead puckered up with a little frown, but before she could say anything Rae beat her to the punch.

"This is something we're doing together. Do you hear me, Molly Skye? Devon proposed to me, and you proposed to Luke. That means we're both getting married. End of story."

Molly shifted uneasily, glancing longingly down the aisles of gowns. "I'm not sure it works like that," she murmured. "And at any rate, that last thing I want to do is steal anything away from your big day—"

"Would you give it a rest already?" Rae plopped down on a velvet chair and folded her arms stubbornly across her chest. "I won't try on a single dress unless you try one on with me."

The two girls stared each other down for a moment, and the saleswoman wisely melted back into a layer of chiffon.

Finally, a little grin spread up the side of Molly's face. "Are you sure?" she squeaked.

"Of course, I'm sure!" Rae leapt back to her feet, excitedly grabbing her friend by the hands. "Allow me to quote a dear friend of mine: This is for your *wedding*. Molly...you're getting *married*!"

The two girls erupted into squeals once more, and the woman rolled her eyes with a little grin and scribbled something down on her clipboard. Millennials. They were so dramatic.

Dramatic, maybe. But choosy.

It wasn't long before Molly had worked the woman into a frenzy. Sending her racing back and forth across the store for new options to try. Ten minutes in, she took off her towering heels just to be more aerodynamic. Ten minutes after that, you could barely see her beneath the pile of fabric in her arms. She was nothing more than a giant cotton ball on legs.

Rae left them to it, wandering up and down the aisles with a dreamy smile on her face. Truth be told, she had never put much thought into her wedding. Probably because she had never been set on the idea of getting married. Not until she met Devon.

Her fingers grazed the edges of the gowns as she floated along.

Up until a few years ago, she'd had a very different idea of where her life was headed. Of how things were going to turn out. Maybe she was going to get into graphic design. Or maybe she'd pursue a degree in journalism. Get a studio apartment in New York, and fill it with ramen and a hypoallergenic cat. Forget about the fact that she'd been orphaned, and set her sights on the future.

It wasn't until she headed off to Guilder—a magical place where her future family was waiting—that everything had changed. That she'd realized it didn't matter *what* you were, so much as *who* you decided to be. That she'd discovered the future wasn't set in stone. That even though the fates dealt you a hand of cards, it was up to you to carve out your own destiny. To fill your life with people you loved. The people who loved you. To write your own story.

She came to a sudden stop, gazing up into the light.

A single dress hung on a curved hook by the window. It had been set slightly away from the others, draped lightly over the frosted glass. Even in stillness, it still seemed to shimmer. Catching every possible ray of light as it beckoned her ever closer.

A soft gasp caught in her throat as she reached out to touch the hem.

It was like nothing she'd ever seen. Like something a fairytale princess would have worn in one of the books her aunt and uncle had read to her as a child.

The ivory lace looked almost too delicate to be real, dancing and swirling in exquisite clouds that covered just the edges of the shoulders, before vanishing entirely to expose the entire back. The bodice was tightly fitted, dusted with constellations of a thousand little crystals. Gems so small that you couldn't even see them, only the incandescent sparkle they left in their wake. A softly shimmering waterfall of silk spilled all the way down to the floor, brushing just the tops of a pair of dazzling slippers that had been placed just beneath.

"What do you think?" Rae whispered, placing a hand on her belly. "Is that the dress we should wear to marry your daddy?"

A flutter of butterflies danced away in her chest as she pulled it off the hanger and disappeared into one of the fitting rooms. Molly and the saleswoman were lost in a deep discussion about handbags, and didn't even notice when she came back out.

For a split second, she couldn't breathe. Couldn't speak. Couldn't move. She froze perfectly still and stared into the floor-to-ceiling mirror, wondering at the girl staring back at her.

Who was she?

A mother? A wife?

What was she?

A hybrid? A president?

The dress whispered against the floor as she swished it back and forth. There was a sudden fluttering in her stomach, and a breathless smile lit her eyes.

I don't know yet...but I fully intend to find out.

"Molly?" She gathered up the folds of fabric in her hand, and made her way further into the changing area. "Are you still back here?"

She had to be. With how many dresses she and the poor saleswoman had stacked up across the floor—it would be a miracle if they could ever get out. Rae heard the fast-clipped flutter of voices, and made her way towards them with a smile.

In the last half hour, the two of them had developed a strange shorthand. One that didn't seem to rely upon words so much as it did gut reactions.

"—and what did you think of—"

"—in certain lights, it comes off as a little too—"

"—that's just what I thought. If it was a little more like the—"

"—yes! That would be perfect! Now if we could just find it in—"

Molly trailed off with a quiet gasp, bringing her hands up to her mouth as a stream of tears slipped down her face. A few feet behind her, the saleswoman dropped the clipboard. But the best friends only had eyes for each other.

"Oh, Rae..." Molly took a step forward. An impressive feat, considering that she was standing in the center of a virtual cupcake of chiffon. All the manic energy that had been propelling her forward melted suddenly as a tender smile gentled her lovely face. "Without a doubt...you are the most beautiful bride I have ever seen."

A breathless shiver ran across Rae's skin as she glanced down at the dress. A wave of emotions lodging squarely in her throat. "You really think it's okay? I know you're supposed to try on a lot of different styles, but this one just—"

"It's *perfect*." Molly had never looked so proud and so overwhelmed at the same time. The girl didn't need Champagne. She was floating on a natural high. "It's absolutely *perfect*." Another pair of tears slipped down her face, and she wiped them away with a burst of delighted laughter. "And here I thought you were going to end up just conjuring a dress..." She trailed off as the saleswoman shot her a curious look. "...from that gigantic closet of yours," she finished quickly, grinning at the look of pained amusement that flashed across Rae's face. "But seriously, you *have* to get that dress."

"It's the one?"

"It's the one."

Rae bit her lip as her stomach did somersaults, imagining the look on Devon's face when he saw it. It was a good thing he wanted to get married so quickly. She could hardly wait!

"Now what about you?" she asked quizzically, giving the gigantic pile of gowns a brief once-over before turning back to her friend standing in the middle. "Are you making any progress?"

"Oh yes," Molly beamed with smug satisfaction, turning back to the mirror. "I think this is going to make a great first outing."

First outing?

They packed up their things. Rae purchased the dress. Right off the rack. Then, together, they headed outside.

Rae glanced back as the glass doors closed, watching as the saleswoman fell onto the couch in sheer exhaustion.

"I still can't believe you actually bought a dress," Molly mused aloud, nibbling on the end of a chip in the corner booth of a diner. "Right off the rack! In one go! And it fit. And you found it all by yourself! I always figured I'd be the one to find you the perfect wedding dress. I figured it'd take months. So much work. So much shopping. Trying on. I don't mean this in a bad way, but you have no style. No pizzazz."

Rae took a swig of soda, and flashed her a grin. "Knowing your track record, you'd have paired it with a beanie."

"Hey!" Molly giggled, tossing a sugar packet her way. "That's only with spy-wear, thank you very much. I happen to recall dressing you for much more formal occasions as well."

"I wonder if that'll ever happen again," Rae said suddenly, stopping the playful back and forth in its tracks as both girls considered the answer.

Molly had been inexplicably reluctant to go home, so the two of them had stopped for a long lunch. Followed by a few more hours of shopping. Followed by a shared batch of fish and chips from one of their favorite diners. The sun had begun to lower in the winter sky, but it felt too good to be out and about to even think of going home. Rae hadn't realized how confined she'd felt until tasting the fresh air of the city. And how much she'd missed hanging out with her best friend.

"I don't know," Molly said thoughtfully. "I always assumed that the lot of us would go back to work. You know, after the whole Cromfield thing died down. But then you were elected president. And then the two of us got pregnant...I don't know where that leaves us now."

Rae fiddled with the edge of the placemat, staring off into space. "I don't know either."

The truth was, she missed working for the Council. As an agent. Not as the president. She missed going out on missions with her best friends. Sparring with them in the Oratory. Gleefully 'forgetting' to complete her paperwork, knowing that her neurotic fiancé would always do it for her.

She missed the adventure. The thrill. The feeling of working hard to develop a talent at something, and then putting those skills to good use. In a lot of ways, she was the last person in the world who should have been elected president. The all-powerful Rae Kerrigan? Sitting behind a desk instead of being out in the field? What a waste.

"Maybe...maybe when the kids are a little older," Molly said hopefully, glancing across the table for validation. "Maybe we can go back together, make the boys babysit at home."

Rae chuckled and raised her hand for the check. She couldn't imagine any circumstance in which Devon would be content to stay home from a mission. But the chance to spend the evening playing with his kid? Yeah—that might just do the trick. "Maybe you can go back into the field." Her smile faded suddenly as the two of them pushed to their feet and headed out the door. "The Council would never allow it for me. It was like pulling teeth just getting them to agree to let me go back out for the royal wedding. And after how that turned out, I don't see them okaying it again anytime soon."

Molly stuffed a quilted hat on her head with a little *humph*. "Why is it even up to them? You're the freaking president. Just do what you want."

The girls wandered leisurely down the street, heading in the general direction of the park between their homes.

"It doesn't work like that, I'm afraid." Rae pushed her hair out of her face with a long-suffering sigh. "Every decision has to go through a committee process, and even I don't have the authority to sway an entire vote. They're depressingly democratic in that regard."

Molly snorted sarcastically. "Maybe you should just pull a Simon. Let's call it a Kerrigan. Declare yourself supreme overlord. Then you can do whatever you want." Her smile faded slightly at the look on Rae's face. "What? Too soon?"

Rae rolled her eyes, smiling in spite of herself. "Yeah...it's a little too soon."

They headed all the way back to their part of the city, ambling along at a relaxed pace, until Molly looked down at her phone in sudden dismay. "Oh crap, is that the time?!"

Rae glanced over curiously. "It's about seven. Why? What's wrong?"

A look of mild panic washed over Molly's face, but she forced it into a tight smile. The two of them were just coming up on the house, but instead of going in she pulled Rae to a sudden stop, holding her tightly by the wrists. "So, I know things have been crazy up in the air lately...but you bought a *wedding* dress today." She stressed the word carefully. "That means we're moving forward, too, right?"

Rae stared at her warily, way too familiar with Molly's crazy schemes to fail to recognize that something was up now. "Yeah..."

Molly's eyes flickered once to the house before returning with that same nervous smile. "So, that means you wouldn't be opposed to a few basic traditions?" Her voice jumped up three octaves, trilling with excitement and nerves. "A little friendly celebration of what's to come?"

Rae braced where she stood, literally angling her body back towards the street. "Molly...what did you do?"

At that very moment, the door to the house flew open and a dozen people burst outside. "SURPRISE!"

Rae froze in place, staring with wide eyes before turning back to Molly.

The tight smile had been replaced with a look of absolute euphoria as the tiny redhead bounced up and down. "I'm throwing you and Devon an engagement party!"

Chapter 10

Only Molly would think she had found the perfect time to throw two of her best friends an engagement party. And only Molly would think it was a good idea to invite both sets of parents.

Rae stared with wide eyes at the odd assortment of people slowly making their way down the walkway, unable to believe they were all in the same place at the same time. It was the clashing of so many worlds and generations, she truly didn't know where to even start.

Julian and Angel came out first, looking especially attractive in a fitted suit and dress, with their arms draped casually around each other. They paused on the top of the steps, sparing Julian from having to walk down, as Luke breezed past them with his father by his side. The commander flashed his soon-to-be daughter-in-law a warm smile before pausing to hold the door open for Beth. She made a bee-line for her daughter, giving Julian a maternal squeeze as she walked by. Simon, her estranged husband, was just a few steps behind. Followed closely by Tristan—his estranged best friend. Followed closely by Mary, *his* estranged wife.

It was enough to make Rae's head spin.

Devon was the last one out. He paused at the top of the steps, looking slightly overwhelmed as he gazed out over the impromptu gathering. Then Julian gave him a little nudge, and he jogged briskly meet the girls.

"Hey, babe, not a moment too soon." He gave Rae a swift kiss on the cheek before turning to do the same to Molly. "Molls."

There was a sharp note of accusation to his voice, and she flashed him a little grin. "Nice tie."

His lips twitched up with an exasperated smile. "Well, a tie seemed appropriate. Given that we seem to be hosting a party."

"*You're* not hosting it," she said quickly. "*I'm* hosting it. Your only job tonight is to sit there and look pretty and try not to get too drunk."

Rae bit her lip, while Devon raked his hair back with a grin.

"You sound like Jules' and my old handler."

"I'm *serious*, Dev—"

He held up his hands with a look of supreme innocence. "I will look pretty and try not to get too drunk." But as she grinned and darted into the house, he couldn't help but add, "Although I can't promise the same for the rest of them..."

Rae gave his hand a sympathetic squeeze as they gazed out over their suddenly cluttered front yard. Half a dozen awkward conversations were trying desperately to get off the ground, but unless Molly had some serious tricks up her sleeve the evening was going to be rocky at best.

At least no one tried to stab anyone yet...

Her blue eyes flickered up to the porch before returning to her fiancé. "So, I take it you didn't have a hand in this—"

"Oh no," he interrupted quickly. "I was just as surprised by all of it as you. Annie and I were hunting crickets in the back yard, when all of a sudden my mom walked out."

Rae could imagine what a shock that must have been. Devon hadn't had any contact with his beloved mother in years, save for a few months ago when he showed up out of the blue to tell her that he had a fiancé and superpowers. It had gone as well as could be expected.

"Wait a second," she looked up abruptly as his words sank in, "*hunting crickets?*"

He flushed self-consciously, dropping his eyes to the pavement. "...we've been working on her pouncing skills..."

A soft chuckle escaped Rae's lips, one that faded quickly when she saw that Mary and Tristan were standing at opposite sides of the yard. "Well, I guess we'd better get this over with," she murmured as the two of them started heading inside. The smells wafting out of the house were enough to put those fish and chips she'd just scarfed down to shame, and since no one in the house had any particular skill at cooking, she was guessing that Molly had made arrangements to have the entire thing catered. "I'm sure Molly spent a small fortune trying to get everything but the guest list just right."

"Anything for a party." A faint grin flitted across Devon's handsome face, and he reached suddenly for Rae's bag. "Here, let me get that for you."

She jerked it away with such force he looked up at her in alarm. A scarlet blush blossomed in her cheeks as she self-consciously tucked her hair behind her ears. "Sorry, it's just...you can't see it. It's my dress."

He shook his head blankly. "For tonight? Why can't I see it, if you're about to put it on—"

She glanced around quickly before clutching it tighter to her chest. "No, it's my *dress*-dress. My wedding dress."

Devon's eyes shot down to the bag like it had suddenly sprouted wings. His hand dropped at once. For good measure, he even walked on her other side. An odd smile played around his lips. "Ohhh."

She glanced up at him with a grin, a wave of that same fluttering excitement she'd felt in the store flushing her entire body from head to toe. "What do you mean—*oh*? You're the one who said you wanted to get married in a hurry. Have you thought about getting a tux yet?"

"Maybe," he teased. "I might just end up going casual. Or borrowing something from Kraigan. It's important to me that the guy feels included..." He shrugged. "You know, something borrowed, something red."

Rae snorted with laughter, thanking the gods of party planning that he was still out of town. "It's blue."

Devon's eyebrow rose. "Your wedding dress is blue?"

"No," Rae rolled her eyes, "it's 'something borrowed, something blue.'"

"So, you want me to wear a blue tux?"

"You should run that blue and 'going casual' idea by Molly. See how she takes it."

It was unfortunate that their over-enthusiastic friend chose that exact moment to scream at a team of terrified caterers.

A shiver ran across Devon's skin, but he shook it off quickly. "Have you gotten me a ring yet?"

She looked up with a start as his bright eyes sparkled mischievously into hers. *Freakin' A! His ring! I knew there was something I was forgetting.* "Of course I have," she lied smoothly. "And, quite frankly, until I slide it onto your finger, it's really none of your business. So, I'd appreciate it if you stopped asking questions."

"Aw, Kerrigan, you forget again..." He draped an arm over her shoulders with a grin as the two of them headed inside. "...I'm the one who trained you how to lie."

Never before had there been a stranger gathering of people. Most of them had, at one point or another, tried to kill the others. And it wasn't like that was all terribly far in the past. Rae would be surprised if they made it through the cheese course without someone pulling out a gun.

And on that note...

"You don't have any more firearms hidden in the house, do you?" she whispered to Angel as people milled about aimlessly in the living room. "No secret weapons I should know about?"

"No," Angel replied with a strange smile. "No secret weapons..."

Rae shot her a curious look, watching as she tossed back her long blonde hair and took a sip of Champagne. A tasteful yet revealing cocktail dress clung to her alabaster skin, stunning her poor boyfriend senseless every time his eyes flickered anywhere below her chin.

But it was the smile that had Rae concerned. And she wasn't the only one.

"Why are you so pleased with yourself?" Molly demanded, swooping up behind them. "The only thing I asked you to do was fold the napkins, and I'm pretty sure you delegated that to Luke—"

"I didn't say *anything*," Angel interrupted, her eyes glowing with excitement. "Not a single word. Not a single phone call."

Molly blinked in disbelief. "Congratulations super-spy. After all this time, you've finally discovered how to keep a secret—"

"Not a secret. A *surprise*." Angel stood up a little straighter as she glanced around the room, beaming with unmistakable pride. "A *surprise party*. Without me, it wouldn't have been possible."

Rae bit back a smile as Molly stomped away in a rage to finish the preparations. She should have guessed. Relatively speaking, things like this were still rather new to Gabriel and Angel.

Surprise parties. Animated films. Windows without bars.

"And what about you?" She turned to Julian, who was still watching his girlfriend with a dreamy smile. "You didn't see anyone...I don't know...killing anyone else, did you?"

His eyes twinkled affectionately as he threw back his head with a laugh. "Rae, I'm on a *lot* of painkillers right now."

He swayed slightly where he stood, and Rae rolled her eyes with a rueful grin. "Yeah, yeah. The door to the future's closed. I get it."

At that moment, a deafening gong shook the entire house.

Rattling the silverware, micro-fracturing the glass, vibrating through people's very bones. Rae, Tristan, and Devon, the people with enhanced hearing, winced in unison—as if they had been struck upside the head, while Annie whined and hightailed it upstairs to hide beneath the bed.

Molly emerged a second later, looking nothing short of delighted. "Dinner is served!"

With no small amount of trepidation, the gang followed her into the dining room. Only to stop immediately in their tracks.

The place had been transformed.

In just the few short hours that Rae had been out shopping, followed by another half hour of cocktails and chit-chat, Molly had somehow managed to create a winter wonderland right there in the living room. Most of it had been delegated to professionals, of course, but the entire thing had Molly's electric little fingers all over it.

Explosions of ivory flowers covered every available surface. Dripping out of vases, and trailing along the banister. Rae's favorite bouquet had been strategically placed in front of a picture of her, Molly, and Devon, angled so that he was blocked out and only the girls remained. The table was set with starched linens, sparkling silver beneath the light of a crystal chandelier, and a thousand little twinkle lights peeked out from every corner, filling the room with an ethereal glow.

On the wall, a tasteful banner was mounted. Weaved in sparkling silver thread.

Congratulations Rae (and Devon)!!!

Yep. This had Molly's fingerprints all over it. Right down to the trio of ice sculptures that were standing in the corner. At least, Rae hoped they were ice sculptures. Realistically speaking, there was no telling what Molly might have done to the caterers.

For a moment, everyone simply stood there, stunned. Even the ear-shattering gong seemed to have been forgiven. Then, at the same time, everyone in the room turned to the happy couple.

"Congratulations, sweetie," Beth said softly, staring at her daughter with a tender smile. "I can't begin to tell you how much it means to me, to see you so happy and so in love. I am so unbelievably proud of the both of you." Her breath caught in her throat. "Andrew would be, too."

Rae's eyes misted over as Devon wrapped a strong arm around her waist. She wasn't expecting anyone to make a speech, and before she could begin to recover from her own mother's words Devon's mother stepped up to the plate.

The woman was a beauty. A *stunning* beauty. With an effortless grace, and the kind of face you saw in picture books growing up as a child. She swept confidently towards the center of the floor with Tristan's eyes trained on her every move.

"Rae, we've only ever met once. I don't presume to know you well, we simply haven't had any time together. But given the time I *have* spent with you, I can come to only one conclusion." She cleared her throat as the emotions threatened to overwhelm, and without thinking her husband walked forward and took her by the hand. The two locked eyes and shared a fleeting smile. "You're a woman worthy of my son," she finished simply. "I can give you no greater compliment than that."

Devon kissed Rae on the forehead before releasing her and crossing the floor to his mother. They embraced in a tight hug, separated by about a foot's difference in height, before she pulled back with a fond smile and pushed his long hair out of his eyes.

"You'll have to cut that before the wedding, you know."

The rest of the room laughed quietly as Julian gave Molly a discreet nod. Best to end to the speeches with the mothers. The last thing anyone wanted was for Simon Kerrigan to give it a shot.

"Shall we sit down for dinner?" Molly asked sweetly, ever the gracious hostess. There were murmurs of assent as people settled themselves around the huge table.

To be honest, it wasn't nearly as awkward as it could have been.

Luke, one of only two people without any ink, was seated next to Simon. A choice that might have been strategic, but the guy was so damn charming you'd never know. Devon's parents sat together, which seemed to surprise Devon but please him at the same time. And the rest of them divided up the remaining space. Leaving only a single chair left open.

"I'm going to kill him," Molly murmured as conversations started up and the food was passed around. "I specifically told him to get here at seven."

As if on cue, the door opened and closed, sending a wave of chilled air into the cozy dining room. A second later Gabriel appeared from around the corner, holding a bottle of Champagne.

"You made it!" Rae greeted him enthusiastically. Even Devon nodded a warm greeting as Angel flashed him a grin. "I was worried you might not come."

"And miss all this?" His eyes flickered briefly around the table before returning to hers with a crooked smile. "Not a chance."

He set the Champagne in the middle of the table and greeted Beth, circling back around to give Rae an ostentatious kiss on the cheek. Devon smiled and started spinning his steak knife between his fingers, while Gabriel took the opportunity to murmur discreetly into her ear.

"It's an...interesting table you've got here."

"Right?" She snorted under her breath, and nodded to the empty chair. "It wouldn't be a true Kerrigan family get-together unless there was a chance that someone might up and die."

When he didn't say anything she glanced over her shoulder, only to see him staring at the chair with a look of cold disbelief. "You have to be fucking kidding me..."

It didn't take a genius to see what the problem was. The only chair available happened to be directly across from Rae's father. A man Gabriel would have gladly beaten to death, even before he'd recently tried to steal Gabriel's tatù.

"Molly," Rae muttered under her breath, "can't you do something?"

Molly turned her head and gave Gabriel a saccharine smile. "No, I can't. Maybe if he'd showed up *on time*, he wouldn't be in this situation."

Rae tried to interject, but they only had eyes for each other.

"No, it's fine. This is exactly where I want to be," he answered bitingly. "At Rae's *engagement* party. Sitting across from her *father*."

Most people would have visibly recoiled from the acid in his voice, but Molly only grinned. "It's settled then." She pushed out the chair, and cocked her head towards it. "Just don't play footsie with him, and you'll be fine."

Gabriel's eyes narrowed like he was seriously considering saying something he would regret, but in the end he forced a tight smile and settled himself down. Simon glanced over immediately but Gabriel turned to Julian instead, acting like the man sitting two feet away simply didn't exist. "How're you feeling?"

An interesting question, seeing as the psychic was having a hard time holding his fork. After a few seconds of trying, he set it back down again with a wistful sigh. "Oh, you know. Like I got stabbed."

On the other side of the table, things weren't going much better. While the adults were clearly making a supreme effort to try to get along, the scars between them ran too deep to ignore.

"I think I met you once," Mary was saying to Beth, leaning across Tristan with a friendly smile. "It was years ago. Tris and I ran into you and a friend at dinner."

"That's right," Beth's eyes softened at the memory. "The four of us couldn't have been much older than the kids are now. Andrew hadn't even gone to work at the school yet."

"Andrew?"

"Her husband," Tristan explained softly. "He recently passed away."

Mary retreated at once, offering a sincere condolence. But Tristan's quiet words had caught the attention of someone else as well.

"Your *husband*?!"

For a split second, the table fell dead quiet. Utensils froze in place as everyone tried to avoid looking at the epic staring match between Beth and Simon. Not the easiest thing to do.

"This whole time," Simon breathed, "I always knew the two of you were very close, but I never imagined…" His eyes flashed with soft menace. "You actually *married* him?"

A cold chill ran up Rae's spine as everyone's eyes flashed back to her mother. People weren't even pretending to be minding their own business anymore; many of them were starting to look seriously nervous. Lately, their group conflicts had tended to end rather explosively. Literally.

Tristan saw the direction things were headed, and was quick to intervene. It helped that he was sitting on Simon's other side, fencing him in with Luke. "You're not going to get anywhere at this table by hating Andrew Carter," he warned in a voice so soft that even Rae and Devon could barely hear. "You were dead, Simon. Let it go."

Wise words, but Simon was in no position to hear them. He jerked compulsively, like he was about to spring to his feet right then and there, but never made it off the floor. It wasn't until Rae glanced discreetly beneath the table that she realized Tristan had him in a death-grip.

The tension in the air was palpable, and linen napkins were laid casually aside as everyone around the table braced themselves in whatever way they could. Julian's eyes flashed white to check the future, Molly's hands glowed blue with static energy, and Devon pushed his chair nonchalantly back a few inches, ready to leap over the table and intervene at a moment's notice.

But Beth didn't look remotely on edge. In fact, she was staring up at Simon with a strange fire burning in her eyes. A heroic defiance. One in which she took both vengeance and pride. "Of course I married him. He was the only man I ever truly loved." As if these words weren't cutting enough, she dug the knife in deeper. "He died to save your daughter's life. Funny how that works, isn't it? One man saves her, while another condemns her with his every breath." Her eyes flashed ice-blue as she looked him up and down. "Tell me, Simon, which one was the real father?"

Someone's going to be killed tonight. Rae sighed.

The room went quiet. Dangerously quiet. The kind of quiet that threatened to suffocate everything in its path. Knuckles whitened, bodies braced, as the entire room held its breath.

Until, all at once, a quiet chuckle echoed through the air.

Rae turned in shock to Gabriel. It was like he couldn't control it. He was still grinning as he reached forward and took a swig of his Champagne. Their eyes met and he flashed her a wink.

"*Now* I'm having a good time..."

As ironic as it was...those happened to be the magic words.

The moment passed.

The tension eased.

And, slowly, helped along by an insane amount of liquor, people began to break down those epic walls to try to talk with each other once more.

"Surely it can't be that bad." Simon set down his glass of whiskey and surveyed Luke with a quizzical frown. "I couldn't imagine—"

"It is," Luke reassured him with an intoxicated flush. "I'm pretty sure there's even a Simon Kerrigan Halloween costume. You're a legend, man. A scary, freaking legend."

Simon absorbed this with a thoughtful expression as Tristan shook his head with a long-suffering smile. "The only word he heard in that whole sentence was 'legend.'"

Meanwhile, on the other side of the table, Devon and Rae were having issues of their own.

"I can't believe you're trying to talk about this now!" he hissed, glancing desperately around the table to make sure they weren't being overheard. "You're not even the one who's drunk!"

Rae bit back a smile, cocking her head playfully to the side. "Oh, I think now's *exactly* the time to talk about it. Of course, you could always just admit you're hilariously wrong and surrender now."

For the last few weeks, the soon-to-be newlyweds had found themselves in a rather difficult position. Difficult in that Devon was *extremely* hesitant to have sex now that Rae was pregnant. The actual logic and science behind the concept didn't matter. He had convinced himself that he would somehow hurt the child. Or at the very least, send it into years of therapy.

"*My dad has superhuman hearing,*" he mouthed with a glare, unwilling to put any sound behind the words.

Rae lifted her eyebrows in surprise, like she had completely forgotten. "Shall we ask him, then? He's a father, he'll know the answer."

She lifted her hand to get Tristan's attention, but Devon grabbed it down with such blinding speed that even she was unable to follow. "That isn't funny, Kerrigan."

"You know what's not funny?" she replied, trying her best to keep a straight face. "Sharing a bed for weeks with a man who refuses to touch me."

Gabriel took a thoughtful sip of his whiskey, murmuring under his breath. "I'm willing to step up to the plate, if you need my help."

Devon shot him a deadly glare. "Not now, Gabriel."

Gabriel shot him a crooked grin. "So many jokes, so little time..."

"Fine," Devon snapped, trying his very best to limit the conversation to as few people as possible. "We'll...we'll just settle it once and for all."

With precision aim, considering how much he and everyone else already had to drink, he lobbed a breadstick over the tablecloth, hitting Julian square in the shoulder.

Julian's eyes snapped shut in pain before he looked over with a slow glare. "Recently stabbed, remember?"

Devon nodded quickly, dismissing it in the same moment. "Jules, I want you to check on something for me."

There was a comical moment of hesitation before he slowly met Julian's gaze. The psychic sighed theatrically, he was obviously asked to do this sort of things all the time, before his eyes paled to iridescent white...and then shot *right* back to brown again.

"Dude, what the hell?!"

Devon raised his hands in the air, shaking his head while Gabriel and Rae covered their faces in silent fits of laughter.

"There's a reason for it, I swear!" Devon said quickly. "It's not about us having sex, but if we hypothetically decided we were going to—"

"Dev, you know I love you, but that is SO far over the line—"

"Would the baby be okay?"

The entire back and forth had happened at no more than a whisper, but the words still managed to pack a punch. Across the table Tristan glanced up in surprise, then lowered his eyes with a purse-lipped smile. Whereas Julian merely slid his fingers over his face like he was considering gouging out his own eyes.

"Yes, the baby would be okay."

Rae raised her hands in silent victory, while Devon still looked unconvinced. "Are you absolutely sure? I know you don't want to check again, but—"

"Rae! A vial of morphine, please."

She conjured it at once, placing it in Julian's outstretched palm. "Is the pain flaring up again?"

"There are different kinds of pain," he muttered, shoving it deep into a vein. "Physical pain and emotional trauma. This is a little bit of both. Plus, the mental trauma."

The adults tuned back in just in time to see Julian shooting the drugs into his arm. He flinched at the initial onslaught then visibly relaxed as it entered his system, tilting his head back to the ceiling as all the tension drained slowly off his face.

"You know, Rae, I have to ask..." Simon began slowly. His eyes flickered to the banner on the wall. "Obviously, it's a little late at this point, but did you ever consider Julian instead?"

Rae spat out a mouthful of cider as Devon slowly lifted out of his chair. Julian glanced up with his Champagne halfway to his lips and froze. "What?"

"I meant for the ink," Simon defended himself quickly as Tristan turned to give him a dangerous stare. "Only in terms of the tatù."

"You are seriously unbelievable, you know that?" Tristan tossed his napkin on the table in disgust, reaching for his whiskey.

"Tris, come on. You know how highly I think of your tatù. It's unparalleled." He gestured across the table to the children, the alcohol freeing his words when otherwise he would have kept them to himself. "I only meant...Rae's all-powerful, and Julian's all-seeing. Imagine what a child..." He trailed off once more, falling silent at the look on Tristan's face.

The reactions around the table were priceless. Rae felt sick. Beth looked furious. Devon grim. Gabriel grinning, clearly unsurprised. And Molly was severely judgmental.

Julian merely held out his hand. "Rae, another vial if you please."

The tension shattered again as she slapped it away with a grin. "Not a chance. We almost lost you once already this month."

"What happened to you anyway?" Mary asked curiously, clearly oblivious to the ink talk around the table, probably writing it off to alcohol. Growing up, Julian had spent most holidays with the Wardells in Esher, and that maternal concern remained. "Did you get hurt?"

Julian hesitated a moment, considering what to say, before no less than five different answers came flying back to her from the entire table. "Donated a rib."

"Car accident."

"Mauled by a bear."

"Mugged on the subway."

"Walked into a wall, the clumsy bastard."

Ironically, it was Julian's own girlfriend who gave this final assessment.

There was a beat of silence, before Tristan turned to his wife. "I stabbed him."

Another beat.

Then Mary burst out laughing. Of all the scenarios that were presented to her, she seemed to find this one the most ludicrous of them all.

"Fine," she chuckled, wiping her eyes, "you don't have to tell me."

There was a knock on the door, and Gabriel pushed smoothly to his feet to answer. The rest of them began passing around smaller plates for dessert, some kind of delightful-looking cappuccino soufflé. It wasn't until they had already started eating that Rae realized Gabriel hadn't come back.

She got to her feet in a single motion, walking away from the golden glow and sparkling conversation, and out into the much colder hall. It took a second for her eyes to adjust, and then she saw Gabriel standing in the front doorway. Staring down at something on the porch.

"Hey, everything okay?" She walked up behind him, placing a hand on his arm. "You have to try this..."

Alicia was lying on the doormat. Limbs twisted around her like she'd been unceremoniously dropped. Her blonde hair spilling over the porch floor. Her blue eyes staring unblinkingly into the sky.

Rae's blood froze in her veins. She didn't have to use the girl's own tatù to see the obvious.

She was dead.

Chapter 11

"Gabriel." Rae's heart tore from her chest; even she could hear the pain in her own voice.

He didn't move. Not a single muscle. He had frozen still as a statue, staring down at the beautiful girl lying dead at his feet.

"Gabriel."

There was no telling what was going on inside his head. Those beautiful eyes had a way of screaming everything and nothing, all at the same time.

"Gabriel."

It wasn't until the third time Rae said his name that it had an effect.

His body jumped slightly as she tentatively lay a hand on his shoulder, and he took a giant step back.

There was a soft commotion behind them as the rest of the party hurried down the hall to see what was going on. They came to an abrupt stop at the scene, staring in horrified silence as snow fell in the moonlit world around them.

"Please," Molly whispered with a quiet sob, "please tell me she's not...tell me she's not..."

Gabriel's head jerked up stiffly as the rest of them quietly wilted. For a second, no one seemed to know what to do. Then, slowly, Angel knelt down and gently closed the girl's eyes.

Both Tristan and Devon scanned up and down the street from where they stood, listening closely to every sound carried by the winter wind, but they both knew it was no use. Samantha was long gone by now. The girl didn't do anything without a plan. Or without an escape.

"She told us," Luke murmured shakily, holding Molly tight against his chest. "She told us that every one of us would pay..."

Gabriel said nothing; he simply stared off into the snow.

Rae stood numbly by his side. Her heart breaking for him. Her heart breaking for her beautiful friend. The lovely doctor who had saved them all more times than she could count. A schoolmate from Guilder. One of the first to fall. Not the first, but it always felt like that when they lost someone.

Finally, when the silence could go on no longer, Angel gave a quiet assessment. "Broken neck. No signs of a struggle." She pulled in a quick breath, staring up at her brother with a look of quiet devastation. "Gabriel... it was quick."

A surge of life flooded back into him, flashing through his green eyes as his face paled with rage. His sister was on her feet the next moment. Ready for anything. Awaiting his order.

"What do you want to do?" she asked quietly. "We can hunt her down right now—you and me. No need to wait. Just say the word."

Julian's face tightened as Devon stared between them in surprise. However, at this point, Rae expected nothing less. The two siblings had assimilated into the family as best they could, but when push came to shove they were a closed unit. Old instincts came back hard, and when death was literally at their doorstep they had very little time for other people.

Gabriel stared down at Angel, taking momentary solace in her face, preparing to say the same words they'd said a hundred times before...but then his eyes flickered up to Julian.

The psychic was stricken. Staring at his girlfriend like he was dying to reach out to her, to take her out of the city, to lock her away someplace safe. He saw Gabriel watching the next second, and quickly cleared his face. He wanted to become a part of their family, not come between it. "I'll go with you," he said softly, ignoring the gaping hole in his chest. "I'll fight with a gun, stay in the car, and tell you what's coming. Whatever you want. Whatever you need."

Now it was Devon who looked stricken. He took a compulsory step forward, his lips parting in protest, before he swiftly closed them again, staring out at the snow instead.

Gabriel's eyes didn't miss a thing.

They didn't miss the way Molly's hand slipped down to her stomach. The way both Beth and Simon were staring at Rae with a look of abject fear. The way Devon's parents were doing the same thing to him. And Luke's parents to him.

In the end... he almost smiled.

"You can't," he said quietly. "None of you can."

That includes you. Rae wanted to say it. She wanted to scream it out loud. But she somehow knew that Gabriel didn't believe that anymore. That in those fleeting moments in the snow, something had changed.

"None of us stands a chance on our own," he continued quietly, speaking at a fast clip. "It's together or not at all. I'm...I'm going home. We'll make a plan in the morning."

Angel was standing in front of him the next second, blocking his path as her white hair swirled and danced in the flurries around them. "I'm not letting you out of my sight."

To protect him from Samantha? To protect him from himself?

His eyes gentled a bit as they stared down into hers. It was the same argument they'd had since they were kids. The one that always ended the same way.

"Then come with me." He held out his hand, and she slipped hers inside.

As the wind swirled around them, he turned and cast one final look at Alicia. Memorizing the image. Freezing with the pain. Then he and Angel walked into the storm together. Their dark clothes and light hair melting away into the winter snow.

Julian and Devon carried in the body, twin looks of grief on their face. They set her down in one of the downstairs guestrooms, laying her gently across the bed. They would call her parents in the morning. They would take all the necessary steps. However, for tonight, she would rest.

A pair of tears slipped down Julian's face as he squeezed her lifeless hand. In the other corner, Molly was openly weeping. He walked away to comfort her as Devon knelt beside the bed, staring at the beautiful girl who had once been their friend.

"I'm sorry," he whispered, smoothing back her hair. "I'm so sorry."

He stayed there for a few seconds before pushing up to his feet. But as he did, something caught his eye. A little frown flickered across her face as he reached down and tugged a piece of paper from Alicia's jacket. In the shock of finding her body, they hadn't noticed it until now.

"What is it?" Rae asked, her voice heavy with dread.

He unfolded it quickly and scanned down the page. Then he froze.

"It's a message," he answered, as quiet as a grave. "Samantha pinned a message to the front of Allie's coat."

A wave of nausea rose in the back of Rae's throat, but she fought to keep it down. Breathing in through the nose, and out through the mouth. Now wasn't the time to lose her head. Now was the time to be strong. To be presidential.

Even if she was dying inside.

Her eyes narrowed as she forced the question past her teeth. "What does it say?"

Devon crumpled it in his hand, unable to look a second longer. "A time and place. Epping Forest. Two weeks from Friday." His throat constricted, and he took a deep breath to steady himself. "She says she's going to finish it."

The nausea off-balancing Rae's stomach suddenly settled, leaving her awash with cold determination. The devastation at seeing her fallen friend hardened into a chilling rage. "No. We will."

The others nodded and silently filed from the room. Devon glanced down once more at Alicia. He carefully removed the pin from her coat, then left her in peace.

Waiting for her family. Waiting to be avenged.

"I'm going to Guilder."

It was the first thing Rae said when they rejoined their parents in the living room. The candles were burning low on the table. The dessert was melted in forgotten pools.

"Sweetheart, why don't you wait until morning?" A rush of sadness welled up in Beth's eyes as she glanced towards the bedroom door. "Nothing will change between now and then."

But Rae wasn't having it. She wasn't going to spend the night pacing the halls. Crying into her pillow. Surrendering herself to emotions that would only derail. She wasn't wasting a second. If one thing had been made clear tonight...it was that time was the one thing they didn't have. "No."

It was short and clipped. Offering not an ounce of leniency.

Beth glanced down helplessly, and Tristan stepped up to the plate.

"Rae, I know you're very upset," he began gently, "but there's nothing that you can do tonight. By the time you get to Guilder, it'll be two in the morning—"

"Then that bloody Council of mine can get their asses out of bed." She glared around the room, then nodded sharply to Devon. "Let's take your car."

"I don't think that'll be necessary." Commander Fodder came into the room, slipping his cell phone into his pocket. Rae hadn't even realized he wasn't there. "I called Louis Keene the second we found the girl. He and most of the others were already in London. They're on their way."

And that's how it's done. A true president. A true leader.

A quiet sigh of relief eased some of the tension in Rae's chest. Allowing her to step back for a moment, and trust the logistics to someone with experience. It reminded her very much of Carter, and for a fleeting moment Rae wished she could just surrender the whole PC into Fodder's hands.

Leaving her own hands free for other things. Like vengeance.

...and making funeral bouquets.

"Thank you," she said softly, swaying as the adrenaline began to ebb, giving way to the horrified shock just beneath. "I should...I need to get ready for them."

Without another word, she flew up the stairs to her bedroom. Leaving everyone behind. She had only just made it inside when that crumbling composure left her. When her clenched teeth tore open with a gasp and she screamed silently into her hands.

A torrent of hot tears poured down her cheeks as she sank where she stood in the middle of the floor. A thousand memories attacked her from every side. A thousand images of Alicia's beautiful face. Laughing. Studying. Walking across the stage at graduation.

The door opened and closed silently behind her. The floorboards creaked as she reached into her pocket and pulled out her phone.

"What are you looking at, honey?" Beth's gentle voice eased into the silence. Warming it through and through.

Rae bowed her head and held up her phone. A hastily snapped picture was lit up across the screen. The picture of a beaming girl flashing a giant thumbs up as she posed next to a certificate. "Aly sent that to me right after she passed her qualification boards. The day she found out she was officially going to be a doctor. Like she wasn't already..." A nostalgic smile blurred the tears in

Rae's eyes as she remembered. She and Molly had gone out that very afternoon and purchased her the official 'white coat.'

"She sounds like a wonderful girl," Beth said softly, sinking down to the floor beside her daughter, gently rubbing her back. "A wonderful friend."

A choked sob tore its way free and Rae bowed her head as more tears began to fall. "She really was, Mom. She really was."

That's when it suddenly sank in.

Alicia's dead. I'm never going to see her again.

The last shred of hope fell away. That last bracing spark against the dark reality. The room around her darkened as Rae broke down and started weeping into her hands.

As the daughter finally fell apart, the mother came forward to hold her together.

Beth gathered Rae up in her arms, rocking her gently, as wave after wave of grief crashed over her. Time ceased to matter. It couldn't touch them there. They simply sat in silence, one holding the other, until the crying finally stopped.

Once it had, Rae lifted her head to stare at her mother. Feeling suddenly as though all the time in the world would never be enough. "Mom...I'm pregnant."

There was a hitch in Beth's breathing as a little sparkle danced in her eyes. "I know, honey."

Rae pulled back, wiping her cheeks as she stared up in shock. "You do?"

A tender smile warmed Beth's face as she stroked back her daughter's hair. "It takes a mother to know one. No drinking. Over-protective fiancé. A gorgeous glow." She laughed quietly as she remembered. "I had more of the nausea than the glow myself."

Rae fell silent, staring down at her hands. It felt like a very long time later that she was finally able to lift her eyes, a whispered truth rising from her lips. "I'm scared."

Beth's arms tightened as she pulled her into a warm embrace. An embrace made all the stronger by the fire that lived inside them. "Of course you are," she whispered. "But there's nothing to be scared about."

"I'm a *Kerrigan*." Another set of tears spilled down Rae's cheeks. "There's *everything* to be scared about. What if my kid turns out just like me? A freak among freaks? Forever haunted by a cursed name?" She pulled in a shuddering breath, shoulders trembling as images from the last few years clouded behind her eyes. "So much death. So much pain. No matter how hard I try to fight against it, the legacy continues—"

"No, it doesn't," Beth interrupted her sharply. When her daughter looked up doubtfully, she took her by the shoulders and stared deep into her eyes. "Your father was hated. You are loved. He tried to take over the world. They asked you to be the president. He could never find happiness, but you—my darling daughter—you did."

Beth was crying now, too. Watching as the hope for her every future slowly came to life.

"You write your own story, Rae. You embrace your own destiny." The two of them locked eyes. "No one can decide what the future holds but you."

It wasn't until the two of them had gone back downstairs that Rae understood the real meaning of her mother's words. That a simple truth, one she'd been struggling with for what felt like her entire life, finally became clear.

The sins of the father are NOT the sins of the son. Or the daughter.

A fierce fire burned inside her. Clearing her eyes, and settling her heart. Beth was right. No future was set in stone. It was what you made of it. And Rae was going to embrace that future with all the strength her mother gave her. With all the strength she'd discovered deep within herself.

All she had to do was stay alive.

As it turned out, that future didn't waste any time getting started.

The representatives from the Council had stayed very late. To say that they were displeased to have discovered that Rae and Devon were getting married was an understatement of supernatural proportions. But it paled in comparison to the news about Alicia.

They reluctantly agreed to let her go into the field, hunting down the evil that plagued them once and for all. They even more reluctantly agreed to her second request. But it was a deal-breaker.

"An official pardon?" Keene stared back at her with wide eyes. "Are you serious?"

Alistair Malcolm, a grisly old battle-axe who could have professionally impersonated Victor Mallins, leaned forward with a snarl. "Gabriel Alden and Angela Cross are the primary suspects in more active investigations than your damn father! Requesting that they just be pardoned—"

"No, no, no, Mr. Malcolm—you misunderstand me." Rae stared at him evenly from her own chair. "I'm not requesting that they *just* be pardoned, but that they also be fully instated as agents of the Privy Council. With all the privileges and protections there within."

Malcolm's eyes bugged halfway out of his head, but unless Rae was mistaken she could have sworn a tiny smile flitted across Keene's face.

"Furthermore, I wouldn't call it a request," she continued, speaking with the same tone of ringing authority she'd heard Carter use so many times. "A request implies room for compromise. Room for change. Feel free to consider this an executive order from your sitting president."

"An executive..." Malcolm spluttered and cursed, trying his best to appear rational in what he clearly took to be an absurd situation. In his defense, it didn't help that he was sitting next to a dripping recreation of the David. "We will...we'll consider it."

Rae smiled. The kind of smile that wasn't really a smile at all. "You'll do more than consider it. You'll make it happen. *Now*." She pushed abruptly to her feet, effectively ending the meeting. "I expect the paperwork to be sent over tomorrow morning."

Malcolm seemed incapable of basic speech, so Keene simply steered him gently towards the door, flashing Rae a little wink as he passed by. "Yes, ma'am."

The second they were gone she collapsed into a chair at the dining room table, all her reserves of emotional maturity running dry. It didn't help that the rest of her friends, the Council's legendary heroes, were currently trying to unstick Annie's tongue from an ice sculpture, armed with a tub of peanut butter, puppy aspirin, and a hairdryer.

Rae didn't think that anyone else was even left in the house, until Luke's father walked out of the shadows and pulled up a chair. They shared a quick smile, blowing out the tapered candles on the table before the cloth caught fire. Then they simply sat back in silence. Lost in thought.

"Carter was always so protective," he finally murmured, gazing out into the darkness.

Rae looked over in surprise. By this point, her every movement was exhausted. Her every emotion stripped raw. The last thing she expected was to have a conversation about Carter. "I'm sorry?"

"I never understood it," he continued in that same quiet voice, eyes so far away it was like he was talking to himself. "I've never seen anyone capable of what you and your friends have done over the last few years. Never seen anyone so resilient, so resourceful, so strong. How could he look at you and feel protective? You seem the last person in the world to need it. But now I understand..."

Rae's breath caught in her chest as he turned to look her in the eyes.

"When I first met you, I saw a broken young woman. An unwilling symbol of the revolution. A mere child forced reluctantly into a position of great power. Today, I see the same thing. A tired, hurting, young woman. The unwilling symbol of an entire government. But still...willing to try." He shook his head thoughtfully, gazing at her in the soft light. "It's time to give you a normal life, Rae. You've earned it a thousand times over. All of you."

The dining room fell silent once more, and he left shortly after. Rae sat there until Devon took her by the hand and led her up to bed. She wasn't sure how much either of them slept, but it was enough just to lie there. Safe in each other's arms.

Thinking about what was to come...

Chapter 12

Epping Forest. Two weeks from Friday.

The words looped like a mantra through Rae's mind. She found herself chanting them at odd times under her breath. Reciting them like a litany as she tried to fall asleep. They focused her when she started to drift. Frightened her when she wasn't careful. But no matter what, they kept her moving. Momentum. That was the game they were playing now. Perpetual forward motion.

She wasn't the only one. The words hung heavy over the rest of them as well. Forcing them each to deal with the ticking two-week deadline in their own unique way.

Angel spent every waking moment at the shooting range. Sending away even the most skilled English gunmen with massive blows to their self-esteem. When it became clear that he wasn't going to be ready for a physical fight, Julian started going with her. After the guns began to bore him, he spent every waking moment combing through the future. Samantha's compulsion on him still held, barring him from seeing her directly, so he scanned the periphery, trying to pick up on any little detail that might prove useful to their cause.

Luke and Devon spent the winter days trying to beat each other to death. In a cheerful sort of way. What started out as a friendly competition, soon flared up into something that would have looked more at home on a Marvel movie set than it did in Rae's backyard. Devon's skills were truly unparalleled. They had yet to meet their match in a fight. But Luke had grown up fighting without a tatù. He thought differently, moved differently. And was constantly catching Devon off guard.

The two of them said they were merely 'training,' just to appease their watchful fiancées, but the stakes had risen a little higher than all that. It wasn't long before they stopped betting money, and started betting other things. Like property. And cars.

The girls, on the other hand, spent most of their time indoors. Instead of practicing hand-to-hand like the boys—a little difficult seeing as they were both pregnant—they focused on the smaller things instead. On trying to expand what powers they already had, fighting like mad for every excruciating inch. It was exhausting. Thrilling. And terrifying. All at the same time.

One memorable morning, Molly lost control and the electric glow that was usually kept contained to her hands spread halfway up her arms. It was a good thing that Annie was outside with the boys, and Rae was practicing her levitation—so that neither one of them was on the ground to feel the shockwave that followed. Unfortunately, the city of London wasn't so lucky.

Maintenance workers came and left, but still had no idea how one faulty generator could have blacked out eleven city blocks. Guiltily avoiding the furious glares of their men the girls decided to call it an early day, and spent the afternoon flipping through wedding magazines instead.

Kraigan was back, much to everyone's dismay. But, Rae had to admit, they were a little glad to see him as well. The guy might be certifiable, but at least he was on their side. As long as they pointed his crazy in the right direction, there was a chance he might actually do some good.

Which only left Gabriel.

He was the only person in the group who didn't seem to have a go-to coping mechanism like the rest of them. He didn't throw himself into any one activity entirely, but flitted from group to group. One day, he'd be blasting away at the gun range with his sister. The next he'd be asking Julian practiced questions, trying to center his visions. After that, he'd spend some time outside sparring with Luke and Devon, before coming in to work on the ins and outs of metallic manipulation with the girls.

Most days, however, he spent locked away in his apartment. It made perfect sense, given the fact that a psychopath had recently doorbell-ditched his dead girlfriend. However, strangely enough, Rae didn't think that's what had him so undone.

He had liked Alicia very much, and the attraction between them was undeniable, but he didn't know her that well. He hadn't known her that long. When Samantha stole the girl's life, she probably thought she was delivering a kill-shot to Gabriel as well. But, while Alicia's death caused him a great deal of pain, it wasn't the thing weighing heaviest on his mind.

For the first time since coming clean, since throwing in his lot with the group of friends and becoming part of the family, Gabriel felt as though there was no longer a place for him.

At first Rae thought it was for the simple reason that everyone else was paired up. There weren't six people in the gang, there were seven. That naturally implied an odd man out. But it went a little deeper than that. It wasn't about physical attraction— Gabriel could find that no matter where he went. It wasn't even about finding true love, as it wasn't something he craved like the others.

It was about finding happiness.

All of them, every last one, had found a way to shake off the trauma that would have defined them. To burn brighter than the darkness, and open themselves up to the possibility of true joy.

Even his little sister. The white-haired monster he had raised in the ground beneath a cemetery...even she had found her happy ending.

Gabriel still had not.

It was perhaps the only problem in the world that Rae couldn't fix. The only path she wasn't able to follow. It was something he had to find for himself.

Later, it's something he can find later. For now, we have a bad guy to kill. One last one.

Momentum. Constant momentum.

And so, the training continued. The visions progressed. And as the day of reckoning loomed ever closer the family banded together, hoping only to survive.

It was an uphill battle, but perhaps the strangest bit of preparation thus far had been spiritual. However, instead of going to a church, Simon and Tristan had gone to a grave.

Rae had tagged along, more out of morbid curiosity than anything else. But, while she had heard the name, she didn't know the man they were going to see. Didn't understand the profound importance of the visit, until she was standing in front of his grave.

Jason Archer.

It was small, unassuming. Set apart from the rest. But you could tell the importance of the person lying there by the looks on the faces of those still standing.

It was quiet for a long time. With both men staring down while Rae stood a few feet behind them.

Then Simon shot Tristan a sideways grin. "He would've kicked your ass."

"Me?" Tristan looked up in surprise. "Everything you've done over the last twenty years, Simon, and you think Jason would have kicked my ass?"

Simon merely grinned, brushing a rock away from the plot with his shoe. "You left the PC. All his hard work and training gone to waste. Yeah, he would've beaten you to death. With a smile," he added, tossing a wink over his shoulder to Rae. "Jason always did those things with a smile."

She couldn't help but smile in return. As strange as these last few weeks had been, the trip to the cemetery almost felt normal. Reminiscing about the legendary trainer. "He could have done that?" she asked Tristan curiously. "Beaten you in a fight?"

She'd heard the stories about Devon's dad. She couldn't imagine it. He was like Devon, tatù and all.

"Hell, yes," Tristan laughed quietly, "with his eyes closed. Who do you think taught me?"

Simon chuckled appreciatively before shaking his head, a mock frown on his face. "And after all that...you just walked away."

Tristan's smile faded slightly, and he lifted his eyes to the trees. "Yeah, well...I couldn't stay. I couldn't be in the field anymore."

Simon turned to him thoughtfully, hearing the story for the first time. "You chose not to?"

Tristan bowed his head with a nod, letting his dark hair spill into his eyes. He looked very much like Devon when he did that. It was easy to see what he'd looked like at sixteen. "Yeah. After they fired me."

Simon's eyebrows shot up in surprise. "Fired? Tris, the Council worshipped you. They would have never fired—"

"Relocated," Tristan amended. "I wouldn't fire my gun. Didn't do my job." His eyes darkened momentarily, as he stared back at the grave. "Then I started firing it too much." The three of them stood in a charged silence for a minute before he lifted his head with a wry smile. "They gave me the school instead. Figured I wouldn't shoot the students."

A dangerous assumption...Given the volatile history of the school.

Simon obviously seemed to think so, too. "They thought you were unstable, so they forced you to sit behind a desk all day with a loaded handgun? Have they never seen *The Shining*?"

Rae bit down on her lip, sensing it would be wildly inappropriate, but even Tristan softened with a faint smile.

"There were times I wanted to use it. On your daughter, in particular." He cast an apologetic smile over his shoulder. "Nothing personal, Rae."

A few months ago, she'd have freaked out. But now she believed him. She had come to understand his reasons for doing the things he did. For walling himself away. As strange as it sounded, they had been done out of love. "You'd have to get in back of a long line, I'm afraid..."

The three of them laughed quietly, still staring down at the grave. The wind picked up and tossed little bits of ice into the air—a precursor of the storm to come.

Simon glanced once at the darkening skies, lowering his gaze to the tombstone. A look of abject misery came over his face and, for a split second, Rae thought he was going to cry. "I've ruined everything," he whispered. "Ruined it all so terribly. Jason knew all about Cromfield. He only ever wanted me to get away..."

Tristan didn't say a word. He simply hesitated for a moment, clapping a brotherly hand on Simon's shoulder. Simon bowed his head for a moment, overcome with the emotion of it all, before turning in quiet supplication to his friend.

"You know that brainwashing device of mine? Think you could use it on me?"

The words were half-joking, half-tragically serious. Utterly devastated, through and through.

Tristan met his gaze for a moment, then his face softened with a faint smile. "You're not getting off that easily, Kerrigan."

Momentum. Constant, forward momentum.

"Come on, let's go home." He wrapped an arm around Simon's shoulders, leading him back to the car. "It looks like it's going to snow again."

It was an emotional reckoning, but the apologies didn't stop there.

Later that same night, Simon stopped Julian as he was heading up the stairs. "Hey, kid, can I talk to you for a second?"

Julian froze where he stood, his handsome face paling with indecision. He might have forgiven Simon after the man saved his best friend, but that didn't mean that things were any better between them. They hadn't talked since the night they went after Samantha—despite having lived in the same house a good deal of the time, and it didn't look like Julian was eager to change that now. "Why?"

Angel and Rae walked around the corner at the same time and froze as well, staring up at the two men. Without taking her eyes off Simon for a moment, Angel's fingers closed over her gun. Without taking her eyes off Simon for a moment, Rae took it away.

Simon bowed his head for a moment before looking up with a thoughtful frown. "I know there's nothing I can say to make any of this better for you. I know that, because of my actions, you didn't get a childhood. Didn't get a family. It's a sin I can never make right."

Julian stared down at the man, but said not a word.

"But if I were you...I would want to know what happened."

It was, perhaps, the only thing he could have said. The only thing that would make Julian take a step back...before hesitantly walking down the stairs.

He and Simon settled at the kitchen table. Angel and Rae hovered on the other side. Two mugs of untouched coffee sat in front of them, but neither paid them any attention. They had eyes only for each other.

"You may think the first time we met was in the boathouse, after they found me in the factory, but that isn't true," Simon said softly. "The first time we met, you were running around an art gallery in Hungary. You couldn't have been more than two years old."

Julian grew very still. His dark eyes locked on Simon. "I've never been to Hungary."

"You were born there," Simon replied. "Spent your first few years living with your maternal grandfather. A renowned artist named Julian Bányai, your namesake."

It was like a tennis match. The second Simon finished speaking, the girls' eyes flashed back to Julian. But it was a tennis match with only one person playing. Julian was just trying to keep up.

"My grandfather..." He stared down at the table, looking a little lost. "I didn't think I had one. Until my father came back, I'd thought all my family was dead."

Simon stayed quiet, letting him work it out.

"We met at the gallery?"

"You kept knocking over these vases." Simon smiled faintly. "Thought it was hilarious."

Rae's throat constricted as she stared with unspeakable pity at her best friend. All the things that Julian was able to see...his own past was a mystery to him.

"Why were you there?"

Simon sighed quietly. They'd clearly gotten to the darker part of the story. "I was looking for your father. He'd gone missing. Tristan and I were sent to find him."

There was a heavy pause.

"But you knew where he was."

It wasn't a question. It was an accusation. As cold and dark as Rae had ever heard.

"At the time, I didn't." Simon reached down, fiddling with the handle on his mug. "It wasn't until I got back that I went down to the church and saw him there."

"In a cell."

Rae blanched as deep-rooted horror stirred deep in her memory. She knew exactly the place Julian was picturing. She knew exactly the cell. They had seen it together.

"Yes," Simon admitted softly. "In a cell."

Julian pulled in a sharp breath, pushing his chair away from the table. For a minute Rae thought he was going to get up and walk away. But he stayed where he was, gripping the edges of the wood as a war of emotions raged behind his eyes. "I...I don't understand. You hated him so much?" A wave of pain rushed across his face, a pain for which there was no remedy. "The two of you had gone to school together—you knew he had a family, a child. You hated him enough to leave him there?"

"*Hated* him?" Simon repeated in wonder. "No! I loved Jacob Decker! I would have done anything for him. He was one of my oldest and dearest friends."

Julian's lips parted as he shook his head back and forth. "Then..."

Simon sighed again, folding his hands upon the table as he bowed his head. "I tried to save him. Tried to take away his memories. It would be simple, I'd thought. One little injection, and he could go free."

Julian was holding his breath. Sitting on the edge of his chair.

"But he refused to take it. Fought me off. Said his memories were who he was. You, your mother—he'd rather die than lose you."

He sounded like a brave man. He sounds a lot like Julian.

"So...that was the choice you gave him," Julian said quietly. "You left him there to die."

"Julian, I did worse than that." Simon pulled in a deep breath. "I left him there, when you and your mother were still there out in the real world. Without anyone to protect you, should Cromfield decide to come. And he did. A few years later...he did."

By now, the tension in the kitchen was almost too much to take. The very air was heavy with it, sticking in their throats whenever they tried to breathe.

"I wasn't there when it happened," Simon murmured. "I only know what Jennifer Jones told me later. People came to your mother's house in Budapest. They'd found out about her somehow, and I'm sure they were coming for you. Your father could have seen it coming. Your father could have stopped it from happening...but he wasn't there."

A tear slipped down Julian's face. Followed by another.

"They chased her up onto a bridge. High-speed car chase, Jennifer said. But they had years of training, and Lili had none. The car went over the railing, and fell a hundred feet into the river below. They found the wreckage the next day. Said there were no survivors."

When Simon first saw Julian, Rae remembered that he had been surprised. Well, of course he was. He thought Julian was dead. That he'd drowned in a river in Hungary.

The story was abruptly over. But the damage left behind was permanent. The scars that remained could never hope to heal.

Julian had frozen very still. It looked like he was hardly even breathing. But, strangely enough, when he finally looked up it wasn't at Simon. It was at Angel instead.

"So, you knew my dad?"

Rae turned around to see not just Angel shaking her head, but Gabriel standing in the corner. He had wandered in unnoticed during the story, and was leaning silently against the wall.

"No, I didn't," Angel answered quietly, her eyes shining with unshed tears. "If he was as powerful as you say, then he was kept in one of the back cells. I was never allowed to go back there. Only Gabriel was."

Julian turned his eyes to her brother, but Gabriel shook his head.

"I never knew your dad," he preempted. "I heard a man screaming. Then he stopped. They all stopped, eventually. I didn't know his name."

A violent shiver swept Rae from her head all the way to her feet. It was like a grisly chapter had unfolded right there in the kitchen. A dark door had opened, one she'd never seen before.

Julian sat like a statue in his chair. As pale and shaken as Rae had ever seen him. A part of her was dying to reach out, but he was in his own world. Lost in a place she couldn't follow.

"My father...he could have stopped it." He repeated Simon's words from before. Speaking slowly, like he was pulling them from somewhere deep inside. "He could have stopped...you."

There was a beat of silence, then Simon nodded. "Yes. There weren't many people in the world who could have made that claim, but Jacob was one of them. Your father could've stopped me."

A stream of tears slipped down Julian's face. Unnoticed, and unashamed. "And if he had, then everything would have been..."

There was another pause as Simon Kerrigan died a little inside. "Yes," he whispered, forcing himself to look Julian in the eyes. "Yes, it would."

It was quiet for a very long time. There was nothing that could be said. There was nothing that could be done. Rae completely avoided looking at her father. She thought if she did, she'd be sick. Instead she kept her eyes on Julian, ready to do whatever he needed. To follow his lead.

But Julian simply sat there, staring down at the table. It wasn't until a full minute had gone by that he pushed back his chair and walked out of the kitchen.

The story was done.

Days passed. Time moved ever on. And slowly, ever so slowly, things began to heal.

The little things that could be fixed began to gradually stitch themselves back together. The bigger things that could not...were left for another time.

Before Rae knew what was happening, they had just a week left to go. Whatever individual notions about preparation they had fell fast along the wayside as the gang came together and reverted to the old days. Hopefully, for the last time.

"Move your feet!" Rae commanded, cupping her hands around her mouth as she watched Luke and Devon flying back and forth across the yard. The sun was out, the birds were singing, and the entire afternoon had digressed to a round of high-stakes sparring. They'd even gone so far as to conjure bleachers just for the occasion. It was a brilliant pairing but, strangely enough, Rae was not on her fiancé's side. "You know he's going to swing left, Luke! You've got to counter!"

Devon flashed her a quick grin as the two of them broke apart, each unable to outmaneuver the other. "Have I told you lately that you're going to make a lousy wife?"

She grinned back, leaning back smugly in her chair. "Every day."

"Come on, Devon! Don't let her get in your head!" In a strange twist of events, Molly had actually sided against Luke. Splitting off the couples and dividing them firmly against each other as the bets raged on.

"This next round might be interesting..."

Both girls turned around to glare suspiciously at the handsome psychic smirking behind them. Julian was never allowed to gamble. Although he delighted in dropping ominous hints.

"Ignore him," Molly sneered, pulling out a wad of bills. "He just does it for the attention."

Rae giggled and turned her eyes back front, but Julian leaned back with a knowing smile. "You know, Molls, raising a kid costs a lot of money."

There was a pause as her fingers flipped through the cash. "Yeah, so?"

He shrugged his shoulders, staring innocently across the yard. "You might want to pick a different side is all..."

There was a dull impact, followed by a blur of speed, as Devon temporarily extracted himself from the fight. "Did I just hear that right?!" he demanded. "Did *you* just bet against me?"

The two of them were still locked in a stand-off, when Luke came barreling out of nowhere, knocking Devon to the ground with a single roundhouse kick.

Molly's mouth dropped open as Julian flashed a grin.

"Told you."

"That's not fair!" Devon laughed, pulling himself to his feet. "You can't team up with people in the stands! This is supposed to be between you and me!"

Luke bounced from foot to foot with a devilish grin. "It's not my fault if the psychic says I'll win."

"No, but it's your fault if the psychic causes it!"

Devon launched himself through the air in a blur of speed, the kind of supernatural attack that Luke could never hope to replicate. Half a second later Luke was lying on his back, panting silently as he tried to catch his breath. As Molly cheered wildly in the stands, Devon flipped once in the air and landed on the ground beside him, offering his hand with a smirk. "And let that be a lesson to you..." He trailed off suddenly as something on the ground caught his eye. For a split second he simply stared, before his mouth fell open in surprise. The others turned automatically to see what he'd found, but by the time they looked back he'd already collected himself.

"Dev, you okay?" Molly called.

He glanced up quickly, nodding his head much faster than usual. "Yeah. Fine."

The girls exchanged a glance and Rae leaned forward in her chair, unwilling to let it go. "What was about? What did you see?"

"Nothing," he replied casually. "Piece of trash or something."

Devon had always been a bad liar. At least to the people who mattered most. While the girls started heckling him, and his best friend tranced out to the future, he strode swiftly across the grass and picked something up, hiding it in his hand. A second later, he returned to Luke.

"I think this fell out of your pocket," he muttered, passing it into his hand. "Sorry."

Molly and Rae looked on with curiosity, but Luke had gone pure white. He glanced down a moment at his closed hand before looking up in the stands at Molly. At this point her face clouded with concern, and she and the others raced down to meet him.

"Luke?" she asked nervously. "What's wrong? What did he give you?"

Luke stared down for another second, frozen stiff, seeming to decide there was no way around it. So, he pulled in a deep breath, flashed a shy smile, then slowly opened his hand.

A breathtaking diamond ring sparkled in the air between them.

Molly's mouth fell wide open as Rae and the others melted back a few steps—staring with breathless astonishment as he dropped down onto one knee. "What...what is that?" she gasped.

His eyes twinkled as his face softened into a tender smile. "It's a ring, my love."

Rae bit down on her lip with a grin as Devon whipped out his phone to discreetly begin filming. But Molly's grip on the world seemed to have been temporarily misplaced.

"But..." She trailed off, staring in astonishment. "How long have you been carrying it?"

Luke grinned, staring up at her. "Oh, you know...about a year."

Even the guys melted a little at that one.

"A year?!" Molly shrieked, her little shoulders trembling up and down with fast, shallow breaths. "Why didn't you give it to me?!"

Luke chuckled quietly. Everything about this moment was clearly not what he had in mind, and yet Rae couldn't help but think it was absolutely perfect. "I wanted to. I tried a million times to think of how to do it—but nothing ever seemed good enough. Plus, we were saving the world a good portion of the time..."

The others nodded practically. It was true.

"And then—you asked me." He laughed again, shaking his head, wearing a twinkling smile. "I didn't know what to do. How could I give it to you then?"

Molly tried to answer, but for once the girl who could never stop talking was stunned into silence. Her hands lifted slowly to her face, but she merely stood there. Trembling from head to toe.

Fortunately, Luke didn't need a long answer. He just needed a single word.

"Molly Elizabeth Skye, will you marry me?"

"Call everyone! Everyone in your phone! Call them right now!" Molly giggled, and shrieked as Luke lifted her up and spun her round and round. They had made it inside, barely. The soon-to-be married couple was completely unable to keep their hands off each other. "Devon, are you calling? I don't even see you getting out your phone! You guys need to call *everybody*—"

She broke off with another breathless gasp as Luke grabbed her face with his free hand and forced it down for a kiss. All conversation paused for a moment, and people watched with fond smiles as she returned it full force, wrapping her arms around his neck.

...then she wrapped her legs around his waist.

"Okay, okay, that's enough." Devon swatted at her ankle. The big brother in him was unable to stand another second. "We'll send out calls to everybody, don't worry. Just keep your clothes on."

"Make sure Julian's the one to call my mother," she said quickly, releasing her death-grip on Luke long enough to fire off another command. Her fiancé gazed up at her curiously, and she rolled her eyes. "He's the only person who can get her to make any sense."

The joyous celebration raged on for the next few hours. Beth drove up from Kent just to offer her congratulations in person, and Commander Fodder looked so happy he could cry. It wasn't long before the entire group was settled around the table for dinner. Rolling their eyes as Molly went smugly from chair to chair, forcing everybody to gawk at her ring.

"Where's Gabriel?" she demanded when she came across an empty seat. "I swear on everything good and holy, that boy's never there when you need him to be!"

Angel glanced up with a slight frown. "He should be here. I texted him over an hour ago."

The rest of the group returned to the celebration without another thought, but Rae stayed rooted to the spot, staring into Angel's worried eyes. Time itself seemed to slow down as a creeping feeling of dread swept over her body.

But it wasn't until her eyes swept around the table that she noticed the only other empty chair. "Where's my dad?"

Chapter 13

"I'm telling you, Rae, he couldn't possibly be here! This entire place was shut down!" Devon raced into the darkness after her, staring in dismay as she flew down the pavement, past the signs warning against trespassers, and leapt over the tall chain-link fence. Angel had flown off in her own direction, but Rae hadn't slowed down since tearing out of the house just twenty minutes earlier. At this point, he had no choice but to follow her.

"He's here," Rae muttered under her breath. "I know it."

The abandoned storage unit stretched before them. Ominously quiet, like some sort of a ghost town. It had the same peeling paint and faded lettering as it had fifteen years ago, when Rae had seen it in her father's mind.

So, this is it. The place where Simon Kerrigan played all his deadly little games.

"Honey," Devon leapt to the ground beside her, panting slightly to catch his breath, "the government shut this place down. It's been hollowed out. There's no reason they'd be here."

"He's *here*, Devon," she said firmly. "I can feel it."

Just a second later, her suspicions were confirmed.

A tortured cry rose up from one of the deserted buildings, echoing briefly before getting lost in the cold night. Rae and Devon froze dead still, their eyes locking onto the same building.

One scream to freeze them. Another to bring them back to life.

They sprang into action in perfect unison. Feet barely touching the wet pavement as they flew across the empty lot, kicking down the door as they raced inside.

It was worse than anything Rae could have imagined. A literal nightmare come to life.

Gabriel was lying face-down on the floor, writhing in absolute agony. Her father stood over him, a bloody syringe still clasped in his hands.

"NO!"

She dove to the floor just as Devon launched himself at her father. There was a brief struggle, but only a second or two later Simon was pressed up against the wall, with Devon's hand wrapped around his throat, squeezing the life slowly out of his eyes.

She wanted to watch. She wanted to watch it happen.

But there were other people who required her immediate attention.

"Gabriel," she gasped, running a helpless hand over his back. "Gabriel, what did he—"

Another scream ripped its way out of him, doubling him over as he cringed and trembled on the floor. There were five wide gashes on either side of his face and his nails were bloody, like whatever was hurting him he'd tried to literally claw out of his head.

This can't be happening...

His head snapped back with another feral cry, and Rae felt like she was losing her mind. She didn't know anyone could scream like that. She didn't know Gabriel could scream at all. She had seen him shot. She had seen him tortured. She had seen him beaten to the brink of death.

It didn't hold a candle to what she was seeing now.

"Gabriel, please!" she cried, trying desperately to keep hold of him as he thrashed violently upon the floor. "Tell me what he did! Tell me so I can fix it!"

Tears streamed freely down his face as he pressed his forehead against the floor, trying desperately to catch his breath. He clenched his teeth together to brace against the pain, but when another wave shook through his body a heartbreaking whimper escaped his lips.

"I can't..." he panted desperately, wrapping his arms around his stomach like he was being torn in half, "please...I can't..."

Rae lay beside him, holding his hand tightly in her own. "You can't what, sweetie?" she pleaded. "Tell me how to help you!"

"...no more...enough..." he begged, crying out into the floor. "...*Simon*..."

Hearing her father's name was a bolt of lightning, propelling her to her feet. She blurred across the room in an instant. Screaming from just inches away. *"What did you to do him?!"*

Instead of waiting for an answer, she punched him full in the face. Then kept punching him. Harder and harder every time.

"What did you do?!" she shrieked again, drops of blood flying off her knuckles. "Answer me, or I swear on his life, Simon, I will KILL you where you stand!"

A breathless sob choked Gabriel's voice as he reached towards them. "...no..."

"ANSWER ME!"

Devon loosened his grip just enough to allow Simon to speak, but he did so with the greatest reluctance. One wrong move, and he'd break the man's neck.

"He came to me," Simon gasped, spitting out a mouthful of blood. "He wanted me to give him the serum I developed. The one to help him enhance his powers."

"YOU'RE LYING!" Rae struck him again, prepared to keep on doing so until there was nothing left. But just as she raised her fist, a breathless voice called out from behind her.

"...Rae, don't..."

She whirled around to see Gabriel reaching towards her. He'd managed to pull himself up to his knees, but the pain seemed to be getting worse, not better. Every breath was agony, and every word was through sheer force of will.

"He's not lying..." he gasped, lifting a hand to his head as the pain stunned him senseless once more. "I...I came here on my own—"

Another scream tore through him, and he fell once more. Completely lost to the world as he grasped desperately onto the concrete and begged the higher powers to let him die.

"*Rae*." It was Devon this time, glancing over his shoulder with a look of fractured indecision. "You heard what he said. We can't—"

"No!" she yelled. "Simon is *doing* this to him! Look where we are!"

"But why would he have—"

"It doesn't *matter*, Devon! *Look around you*!"

They could have gone on forever, but Gabriel cried out once more and Simon threw himself against Devon's restraining arms. "Let me help him! He can't take much more!"

Gabriel's body convulsed, and he raised his voice to a deafening shout.

"RAE, HE'S GOING TO DIE!"

Time stopped for a moment as she stood there, staring down at Gabriel's body, wondering who to trust. Then a cold tremble swept across her skin, and she nodded.

The second Devon released him, Simon raced across the floor. Not to Gabriel, but to a series of metallic cupboards stacked against the wall. He started frantically punching numbers into a keypad, and the door popped open and he snatched up a colored syringe.

He was back across the room the next instant, diving to the floor and pulling Gabriel up onto his knees. Gabriel moaned quietly as he was lifted, but held perfectly still as Simon pressed the needle into his body. A second later, the trembling lessened. A second after that, it stopped.

"Thank you," he breathed, dropping his head back in sheer exhaustion as Simon lay him gently down on the floor. "I'm sorry, I...I couldn't do it."

"Don't be sorry," Simon murmured, reaching down to take his pulse. "No one could have started with the dose you did. You're lucky to be alive."

"Lucky." Even lying half-dead on a cheap linoleum floor, Gabriel Alden still managed a faint smile. "Right."

It was like stepping into some kind of alternate universe. A parallel dimension where anything could happen and none of the rules applied. Rae and Devon flashed each other a look of utter astonishment before turning back to the others.

"What the *hell* is going on?" Rae demanded.

More than the screams and the dying, she couldn't get past the fact that Gabriel had just let Simon take his pulse. That he'd let Simon touch his bare skin.

Gabriel glanced up swiftly then pushed shakily to his feet, grabbing automatically onto Devon when he offered an arm for support. "When I was younger, I remember hearing Cromfield talking about some kind of serum that your father was developing. He was jealous. And proud. Supposedly, it was designed to enhance a person's ink. Let it progress faster than was natural." He pulled in a sharp breath, still reeling from the aftershocks. "I went to your father. Asked him if it was true. Asked him to give it to me." His eyes flickered to the syringe on the floor. "We came here and tried."

There was a beat of silence. Then a fierce voice shot through the air.

"You stupid son of a bitch."

Rae turned to her fiancé in shock. He had taken a step away from Gabriel, forcing him to stand on his own, and stared him down with a look of violent rage.

"You could have died. Do you realize that?"

Gabriel hesitated for a moment, a little taken aback. Out of all the people standing in the room, Devon was the last person he'd expected to confront him. When he finally answered his voice was quiet, though he tried to make it strong. "I had to try. I had to do something—"

"You could have *died*."

At first, Rae didn't understand why Devon was so angry. Yes, Gabriel took an impossible risk by coming here. And yes, they were all as furious as they were afraid. But this...this felt like something different. A moment later, she realized why.

"You don't get to play around with your life anymore. Don't you get that?! You don't get to take those kinds of chances!" The words rattled the metal walls, shaking them all to the core as Devon's eyes burned a hole into Gabriel. "Not after what he did. Not after he saved you."

Rae bowed her head as a wave of understanding crashed over her. On the other side of the room Simon was watching them all very carefully, a peculiar expression shadowing his face.

Gabriel's face tightened in pain as his teeth clenched together. For a second, he looked ready to knock Devon out cold...if he was only able to stand. "Well, maybe Carter made a mistake."

His quiet retort couldn't have proved a greater contrast to Devon's deafening accusation, but the argument wasn't over. Not by a long shot.

"Because that would make it easier, wouldn't it?" Devon took a step forward, levelling Gabriel with his gaze. "If he was just wrong. If you're an unredeemable asshole, and he made a mistake by saving your life. It would be easier than acknowledging what he did. Than living up to it."

Rae had never seen Gabriel Alden lose a fight. But she'd never heard him scream before either. His lips parted uncertainly, but before he could say a word Devon spun on his heel and walked right out the door.

"I'm going to pull the car around," he called back to Rae, shaking his head in disgust. "Do what you want with these two."

The door slammed behind him, leaving a chilling silence in his wake. The three of them stood there for a moment, each trapped in their own little hell. Rae squared her shoulders firmly and turned to her father.

"Find your own way back."

Simon met her eyes for a split second, then he nodded. The next second he was out the door, blurring away into the night with the speed of a fennec fox.

And then there were two.

Rae slowly turned back to Gabriel, and he looked back up at her. For a moment, neither one of them said anything. Then she found herself echoing a recently shouted phrase. "You son of a bitch."

She hadn't yelled the words like Devon had, but he flinched all the same. It was a rare moment that Gabriel would show remorse. It was something that had been omitted from his childhood programming, and had only returned with deliberate personal growth. But he certainly looked sorry now. His entire face was awash with it.

"I didn't want to die." It was said only a little louder than a whisper, but still seemed to carry through the entire room. "I didn't come here wanting to die."

"I know," she answered softly. She hadn't thought he did, but it was still good to hear him say it out loud. "Let me guess, after all the shit he's done you told him the only way to make it right was to help you. To give you the serum."

Gabriel shook his head, wrapping his arms protectively around his chest. "No, I told him he could never make it right. Then I asked him to give me the serum."

She wanted to rage and scream. She wanted to shake him senseless. To tear into him like Devon. But at the same time...the only thing she wanted to do was take him into her arms.

She couldn't imagine what it had to take for Gabriel to come to Simon. She couldn't imagine what it had taken for him to have held out this arm.

A scathing reprimand died on the tip of her tongue, but the longer she stood there in silence the less it was required. Gabriel seemed to be taking care of it all by himself.

"He made it mean something—my life. His sacrifice made it worth something." A pulsing light flickered behind his emerald eyes, and for a split second he looked truly terrified. "I don't know what to do."

Rae stared at him for a long time. Long enough that, outside, the snow stopped falling. It was a question without an answer. One he'd have to work through himself in time. In the end, she simply offered her hand.

"Come on. Let's go home."

The car was waiting out front by the time they limped through the door. Devon never took his eyes off the road, and the three of them didn't say a word until they got back to the house. The second they walked inside Gabriel was passed into Angel's waiting arms; Rae and Devon went up to their bedroom and began quietly undressing for bed.

It wasn't until they were settled under the covers, a happily snoring puppy wedged between them, that Devon finally broke the silence. "Sorry I almost strangled your dad."

Rae glanced over in the darkness, then returned her eyes to the ceiling with a shrug. "I almost fractured his skull. You're in good company."

There was a slight pause before Devon spoke again, his voice dropping to half volume. "And sorry I was so hard on Gabriel. I just couldn't imagine..."

"What?" Rae glanced over suddenly. "You couldn't imagine a person shooting himself full of dangerous chemicals just to make himself stronger for a fight?"

The parallels were as ironic as they were frightening.

Devon smiled faintly, but it dimmed the longer he lay there. Finally, he bowed his head with a quiet sigh, spilling his dark hair over his eyes. "No...Carter."

A silent tear slipped down Rae's cheek as she reached under the covers to take his hand. "That was a nice speech you gave. It's a shame he wasn't here to see it."

Devon paused for a moment, staring up at the ceiling with a sigh. "He kind of was...Carter gave that speech to me once."

What?

Rae propped herself up on her elbow, turning towards him in the dark. "He did?" she asked. "When?"

"After my dad kicked me out of Guilder." Devon bit his lip, his eyes drifting back as he remembered. "I was a wreck. He found me in the Oratory, tearing the heads off the mannequins we used to use for target practice. First he made me stop. Then he helped light them on fire."

Rae laughed before she could stop herself. Her entire body relaxed in a wave of bittersweet tenderness as she tried to imagine it. Oddly enough, it wasn't that hard to do. Devon joined in for a moment before getting back to the story.

"He told me that my dad was wrong to have done it, but that I didn't know the full story. Mostly, he just told me that grudges can kill. You hang on to that pain long enough, it will destroy you. The only thing you can do is move on. The only thing you can do is look ahead."

A strange feeling of calm settled on them both as they lay in the darkness, silently holding hands. The words were recounted with such quiet accuracy that Rae could almost hear Carter saying them. She could take fleeting comfort in the distant echoes of his voice.

"He should be here," she whispered, almost to herself. "He needs to be here. He should never have been taken away."

Devon sighed again. "Yeah...but he was." It was quiet for a moment before he suddenly squeezed her hand. "But I know a place where we could find him..."

It was the last thing they did before the fight. And it was something they all did together.

The entire gang stood before the grave. Rae, Devon, Julian, Molly, Luke, Angel, and Gabriel. Beth and Tristan stood side by side. Simon was standing behind them. Even Kraigan had decided to come along, hovering silently on the periphery. The entire unlikely family had come together one final time...with the tragic exception of one important member.

Despite the wintercold, a lone bird in a branch above them started to sing. It was a quiet song. Bittersweet. One that seemed fitting for the occasion.

Rae closed her eyes as she listened, swaying slightly in the breeze.

It was Thursday evening. The day before the reckoning. The day before that final day, where they would fight that final foe...and see who lived to see the weekend.

After so many years, after so many battles, Rae couldn't fool herself. She suffered no delusions as to what was about to come. No matter how hard they had trained, no matter how much they had tried to prepare, she was well aware that some of the people standing around her weren't going to make it to tomorrow's sunset. That, by Saturday morning, those still standing would be making arrangements to put those people in the ground, in a grave very similar to this one.

With the echoes of Samantha's murderous oath still ringing in her ears, it was impossible not to think that she might be one of them. That the culmination of everything that had happened in her life—every time she'd ever laughed, every person she'd ever loved—might have been leading up to this very moment. That she and all of her friends had gathered here for a simple reason.

To say goodbye.

It was too much to think about. Too overwhelming to consider. In the end, all she could do was close her eyes and listen to that little bird. Dreaming of a future that might never come.

"He taught me how to whistle," Julian said suddenly.

Rae's eyes snapped open. The entire gang turned to stare at him in disbelief, while Devon shook his head with a look of strained exasperation.

"It's safe to say he taught you a lot more than that, Jules."

"No. I know," the psychic backtracked quickly. His eyes flickered apologetically down to the grave, before clearing with a simple shrug. "I was just saying...he taught me how to whistle."

Beth squeezed his shoulder, as the rest of them warmed with a little smile.

"He let me borrow his car once," Molly piped up suddenly. "There was a trunk show in the city, and I couldn't get anyone to take me there. He watched me go through every single person in the Oratory before handing me the keys. Told me to have it back by eleven."

Luke nodded thoughtfully, then cocked his head to the side. "Did he know what a trunk show was?"

The others laughed as Molly shook her head with a nostalgic grin. "No. I don't think he did."

There was a slight pause before Beth shook her head, a smile on her face. Her eyes had locked on the gravestone with great tenderness. As if she didn't see the stone, but the man. "That was Andrew. There wasn't a single problem he couldn't solve." Her arms wrapped tightly around her chest. "And there wasn't a thing he wouldn't do to solve them."

The rest of them nodded. Each remembering in their own way.

"He knew I was always jealous of your gift," Devon said suddenly, turning with sudden fondness to his best friend. "I think that's why he paired us up together in the beginning. Thought it might teach me a little humility."

Julian stared at him in shock. "Jealous? Dev, you can...you can basically *fly*." He laughed at the absurdity of it all. "You can't possibly be jealous of clairvoyance."

But Devon merely shrugged with a little smile. "Are you kidding? Jules, I can run really fast. Jump really high. You? You can see the freakin' future. Your mind can do things that I can't...I can't even begin to imagine." He shook his head in honest amazement. "What does it matter to be good at fighting if you can see ahead and stop the fight from happening altogether?"

Simon looked up sharply, a sudden intensity dilating his eyes.

"He saved my life," Gabriel said quietly. The inherent responsibility in the words was written all over his face. But, for once, he didn't look like he was fighting it. Quite the contrary. The longer he stood there, the more he seemed to rise to the challenge. "It's something I'll not soon forget."

He and Rae stared at each other for a long moment before she turned her eyes to the grave.

"He touched us all. Saved us all. The least we can do is make it count."

Without another word, the gathering abruptly ended. One by one, the people gathered reached out to touch the icy stone before heading back to their cars. Beth actually knelt down to kiss it, and Devon helped her up and led her slowly back to the car.

In the end, only Rae remained.

The wind blew gently around her as she stared down at the stone. Unable to stay. Unable to ever fully leave. The rest of them were clear on the other side of the field, but they were in no rush.

Nor were they in earshot. Rae watched them for a moment before turning back to the grave.

"We're really scared this time," she said softly. "All of us. I don't know how to explain it, but this one feels different from the rest. It feels...final."

A chill swept over her, and she pulled in a deep breath.

"One way or another, we're going to make you proud. And Mom will be fine. Don't you worry about that. She's stronger than I ever imagined." A fleeting smile danced across her face. "You should've seen Devon the other day. Shouting out drills like we were back at Guilder. I swear, he sounded just like you..."

She trailed off, staring hard at the stone.

"We're ready. I know that we're ready."

If only that were enough.

"But I wish you were here."

That bird started singing again. Quieter this time. Sweeter. Rae glanced up at it, staring out across the grass at her friends. "I wish you could see the people they've all become. So determined. So...good. No matter how many things beat them down, they keep getting up again. Just like you taught us. Fighting the good fight. Protecting each other. Reaching for a future we might never get to have..."

A single tear slipped down her face as she looked down with a smile. Resting a hand against her belly. Closing her eyes as she whispered the world a silent goodbye.

"I wish we could have had more time. I wish you could have met your grandchild."

Time seemed to stop when she opened her eyes and froze.

What the freakin' heck?!

She froze. They all froze. Everything...froze.

Chapter 14

Simon whirled around in astonishment, unable to believe his eyes.

The wind stopped. The snow stopped. The people standing by the cars stopped moving. It was as if the entire world had been put on pause, fixed in a state of peaceful suspension.

With extreme hesitation, he took a step forward. Then another. Staring around the cemetery with wide, unblinking eyes.

His first thought had been that his daughter was controlling it. That she'd somehow intuited he had been listening in secret behind her—and was preparing to blow him away once and for all with some final wave of power.

But Rae was frozen with all the rest of them.

It's me. I'm the one doing it.

A wave of shock crashed over him and, reverting back to old habits, he glanced reflexively at the warlock tatùed on his arm. It stared back up at him with the same enigmatic expression that it had since he was sixteen. Since it first appeared on his skin and started all this trouble.

He had memorized it within the first week. Could sketch it to perfection every day since. And yet, he had never placed any significance on a tiny detail until that very moment.

The warlock was holding a clock.

Half my father. Half my mother. A hybrid.

His eyes widened as he slowly pieced the mystery together. The part of his past that he had never been able to understand.

The ability to mimic. And...the ability to control time?

It had to be. There was no other explanation.

With a wave of almost blinding excitement, he moved forward and waved his hand back and forth in front of Rae's eyes, waiting with bated breath. She didn't blink. Didn't even flinch. A look of peaceful surrender was frozen on her beautiful face; for a moment Simon actually forgot about the tatù, and all he could do was stare.

"You're going to be an amazing mother."

He said the words aloud. A beaming smile stretching proudly across his face.

If you ever get the chance.

That smile was quick to fade. Replaced instead with a look of profound sadness.

A strange tingling started rising up his body, from his feet to his palms. It wasn't long before it overtook him completely. Centering him with an unfamiliar focus. Grounding him with a bizarre calmness. It was an understanding—a realization—that had never occurred to him before. It was over in a few seconds. Gone before he could pull in a full breath. And yet, he instinctively knew it was the moment he'd been waiting for all his life.

For the first time, Simon didn't care about the powerful ink emblazed upon his arm. He didn't care about the impossible power that had suddenly come into his grasp, or the unlimited possibilities that came with it.

He cared only about the future.

The future that his daughter, and his beautiful Beth, so desperately deserved. The future they longed for with every waking breath. The future that they could only have if...

All at once, Simon knew what he had to do.

Despite the complexity of the ink, the premise was rather simple. If Simon could stop time from moving forward then, surely, he could force it to move backwards as well.

His feet crashed down upon the grass with the strength of a nova, soliciting a soft gasp as he slowly straightened and looked around him.

Winter was gone. Summer was here. But not the summer the world had been expecting. It was a summer that had already happened. Just two years in the past.

Simon gazed up at the side wall of a house. A house he had never seen before, though he instinctively knew where it was. Who it belonged to. After years of studying them, his old case files were burned permanently into his mind. Flashing fresh in his mind's eye.

This house belonged to a certain telepath he had once tortured, to the point of complete mental collapse. After Elias died, it didn't go to the state. It transferred possession to his daughter.

Simon's feet didn't make a sound as he walked over the shimmering glass and peered inside the living room window. Samantha was sitting by herself on the couch. Sullen and bored. Watching a program on the TV. A half-eaten bag of chips lay beside her; judging by the slightly glazed look about her adolescent eyes, she had long since lost sight of the outside world.

Simon took a step closer, reaching into his pocket at the same time. His fingers closed around a cold, metal grip. And in the brilliance of the early evening sun, he pulled out a gun.

One last terrible thing.

He fired two shots in quick succession. Aiming for the back of her head. She never saw it coming. Never had a chance to be afraid. She simply slumped forward onto the sofa, slipping to the floor as a burst of canned audience laughter roared from the television set.

"I'm sorry," he said quietly, stepping back into the light. "You didn't deserve this. But trust me, you would not have liked what you become."

One last terrible thing.

He slipped the gun back into his pocket. Pulling in a final breath of the sunlit air.

And one good thing as well.

A rush of air exploded in his ears as he was tugged out of the light by a power far greater than himself. His eyes snapped shut as the sensation of falling lifted his limbs into the air.

When he crashed down again, it was different than before. Not only was he inside, but the world was cold. Cold and dark as hell.

His eyes flashed to the stone ceiling above him as a series of shouts and screams echoed distantly in the air. There was an explosion of what sounded like gunfire coming from up above, followed by an explosion that shook the very ground beneath his feet.

There were footsteps racing towards him, faster than he could believe. His head snapped up, and the world cleared into sudden focus as he found himself face to face with a man he never expected to see again.

"*Simon?*" Carter screeched to a halt, staring as if he couldn't believe his eyes. "Is that..."

There was a crash behind him as bits of plaster and dust fell from the walls. More screams came from up ahead, and a wave of panic lit his eyes.

"How can this—"

Simon knocked him to the ground with a single punch. Shoving him protectively into the wall as he turned towards the screams coming from the room at the end of the hall. "Sorry, old friend, but this is something I have to do myself."

With only the power of the warlock to help him, with only the instincts of a father to guide him, Simon took off running down the hall. The door had already burst open, and it took him a fraction of a second to make sense of what he saw.

His son, Kraigan, battered and broken, locked in a deadly battle against his greatest foe. His future son-in-law at death's doorstep, bleeding out in the floor. His beloved daughter, looking like her heart was being ripped straight out of her body. A look of abject terror on her face.

And Jonathon Cromfield pointing a gun at Gabriel's chest.

Simon didn't hesitate.

Nor did he regret a single moment.

He'd seen a glimpse of the future on his daughter's beautiful face. Seen the bright promise of tomorrow shining in her eyes.

It was a promise he intended to keep.

With a burst of speed, he threw himself straight into the path of the bullet. Absorbing it into his own body. Shoving Gabriel aside.

The two of them locked eyes for a suspended moment, staring in shock as something passed between them that neither one would ever understand.

Gabriel would never believe it. Simon would never get the chance.

Chapter 15

"Well...this is thrilling."

A burst of sparkling laughter echoed in the air as Devon joined Rae at the end of a long stone hallway. They had been at it for several hours now, clearing the factory, checking the cells, and his lovely fiancée was at the end of her rapidly fraying rope.

"Relax, turbo. We're here."

He stepped back as another member of their party held up a breaking bar, but Rae beat him to the punch. With a look hovering dangerously on the edge of boredom she took a step back, and kicked the metal door with every bit of her not inconsiderable might.

An explosion of dust and grime clouded up in the air around them, and they took a step back.

"There," she said with finality. "Done."

The men behind her chuckled and Devon shook his head, wearing a twinkling smile.

"Did you even check inside?"

A playful grin flashed across her face, and she doubled back with exaggerated patience.

"I was just getting to that part." She stuck her head inside the darkened room, glancing this way and that as her eyes adjusted to the dim light. It was smaller than she'd expected. Smaller than the rest of them had been. Other than that, it was entirely unremarkable.

Except...

As she turned to go, some quiet instinct made her pull back. Her hands wrapped around the iron bars as she gazed into the darkness, struck with the strangest notion she'd been there before.

"So how about it?" Devon called, just as eager to get back into the outside world as she was herself. "Find any monsters in there?"

The moment passed and she turned away from the shadows. It was like someone had one been there. Someone her tatù seemed to know. And yet, it was a wisp of a thought, fleeting and gone before she could figure it out. "Nope. Let's go home."

The two shared a smile as they left the darkness behind them. Walking back into the light.

Epilogue

Rae watched as the flames danced higher and higher into the sky—the flickering reflection burning deep in her eyes. A cloud of smoke was soon to follow, threatening to engulf everything around it. She stood there for a moment, staring, then continued to set the table.

"Devon!" she called, placing silverware neatly onto napkins. "The food's going to burn!"

Her husband glanced up, then hurried across the lawn to tend to the grill. It had seemed so easy when they'd first envisioned it. A family celebration right there in the backyard. No pressure, no fuss. The execution, however, left a little to be desired.

"Don't you wish you'd followed my advice and gone with the caterers?" Molly asked smugly, handing off a pitcher of lemonade before settling down at the table. "Saves *loads* of time."

"It's a barbeque, Molls." Rae shook her head with a grin. "I'm not going to hire a team of caterers to help us make burgers and fries."

Molly shrugged daintily, then squinted up at the smoke. "I at least hope you guys got this place insured..."

Rae swatted her with a napkin, and returned to her work with a smile.

Despite the very real possibility that they would probably end up ordering pizza, she couldn't have asked for a better day. It had been one of those crystal-clear summer mornings, which had cooled into a gorgeous afternoon before sinking peacefully into a glowing, golden dusk.

She had been woken by a gentle kiss from her adoring husband. She had then been assaulted by the over-enthusiastic puppy they'd adopted just a year or so back. And just when she thought her heart couldn't get any fuller, the hallway echoed with the pitter-patter of little feet...

"Aria!" she called as a tiny dark-haired girl darted past her. "What did I tell you about running so close to the grill?"

The girl screeched to a stop, a pair of enormous guilty eyes staring up. Every inch of her nymph-like body seemed to quiver in excitement as she tried her best to hold back a grin. "You said...I should do it carefully?"

Molly snorted into her hand, and Rae pursed her lips to hide a smile.

"Try again, monster."

The girl blushed with a little giggle. "You said not to. Sorry, Momma."

Rae gave her a little wink before waving a hand at the yard. "Off with you!"

She darted away without a moment's pause, grasping onto the hand of the little boy who was running beside her. A little boy with flaming red hair.

"You're trying to stop *Devon's* daughter from running around?" Molly asked, her blue eyes sparkling with a wicked smile. "Good luck."

"I'm trying to stop *my* daughter from playing with fire," Rae answered with a rueful grin. "If for no other reason than to avoid the inescapable irony."

Molly snorted again, stretching back against the table. "Like I said: Good luck."

The yard suddenly exploded with little squeals of delight as the swinging gate opened and a handsome man walked inside. He was holding the hand of a woman just as lovely. A woman who looked like she was just weeks away from having a baby of her own.

"Uncle Julian!"

Aria blurred across the lawn and leapt into his arms. The little boy, Benjamin, was fast on her heels. Julian scooped her up with a grin, then stood there with unending patience as she painted a giant daisy on the side of his face.

When she was finished, he glanced at the reflection in the kitchen window. "Looks like you inherited your artistic talent from your mother."

Rae shot him a secret grin, while her daughter beamed with pride. "Do you think I should do one for Auntie Angel?"

Julian kissed her cheek. "Not unless you want Auntie Angel to freeze you."

Aria erupted in a fit of giggles as Benjamin tugged Julian's coat impatiently. The little man had no time for daisies or other such trivial nonsense. They had serious business to attend to.

"Do the weird eye thing!" he begged as Julian set Aria back on the ground. "Please?!"

With that same unending patience, Julian bent down and looked at the children very seriously. Both were waiting on pins and needles, and both jumped a mile high when his eyes flashed prophetic white. Aria clapped her hands together delightedly, and Benjamin jumped up and down.

"What did you see?! What did you see?!" he squealed.

As usual, he was as frightened as he was impressed.

Julian ruffled his hair with a smile. "I saw you asking again in five minutes."

Before the either child could say a word, he caught them suddenly in his arms. Biting playfully at their little arms, he took turns throwing them high into the air. Their screams of delight echoed in the yard. Breathless with excitement as they flew higher and higher.

Rae watched them with a tender smile.

It was good practice for when his own little girl arrived, in just a few weeks' time.

Julian had already begun sketching her. An exquisite little girl with white-blonde hair and dark, knowing eyes. The most recent of the drawings was currently hanging above her crib. Just waiting.

It wasn't until the kids began to graze the tips of the trees that she and Molly called out at the same time. Julian set them down with a grin and headed over, Angel following by his side.

"Nice daisy."

His hand lifted to the paint, and he glanced back at the children with fond affection. "Thanks. I'm thinking of keeping this one."

It was hardly the first.

Yesterday, when Rae and Devon had gone out for a rare night on the town, they had come back to find Julian passed out on the sofa, Aria tucked safely in his arms. They had come home on similar nights to find his hair braided. His nails painted. The list was endless. On one particularly memorable occasion, they had found the hint of eye shadow still glittering across his skin.

"Just wait," he'd warned when Devon had laughed. "Just wait until it's your turn. And, rest assured, my kid will paint a hell of a lot better than yours."

The two of them locked eyes across the yard, and Devon jogged over with a smile.

"Hey, you made it." He handed Julian a beer, tilting his head back towards his daughter. "Don't get my kid stuck up a tree."

"No promises," the psychic replied with a grin. "Feel free to do the same to mine. You are her godfather, after all."

Devon's face soured with a look of boyish petulance.

"One of *two* godfathers," he muttered resentfully.

Julian lifted his hands innocently.

"It wasn't up to me. Not entirely. I wanted you, but Angel wanted Gabriel. Said that when we go down in a fiery gunfight, she wants him to protect the baby."

Motherhood was going to be interesting for Angel. She was full of things like that.

"So," Rae interrupted excitedly, "Devon told me that you guys finally settled on a name!"

Julian quieted thoughtfully, while Devon clapped him on the shoulder, looking proud.

"Lily, huh?"

Julian hesitated a second before his face brightened with a gentle smile. "Yeah. Time for a fresh start, right?"

Devon's eyes twinkled. "Right."

They shared a fleeting smile, and Julian glanced casually at the grill. "That's about to catch fire."

Devon hurried off to save the food, while Angel followed automatically to freeze the flames.

"So..." Rae bit her lip with a mischievous grin. "How's life in the asylum?"

Julian raked his fingers back through his hair with a tired chuckle.

Two years ago, he and Angel had bought a house on the other side of the park. It was just a minute's walk away from Rae and Devon, and the men swore that if you stood at a certain angle at a certain time you could actually see the other through the trees. It was a lovely cottage. Very similar to the one Rae was living in herself. Except that it wasn't always just the two of them.

Since Gabriel sold his apartment, he'd made a habit of staying with them whenever he was in London. Meaning that Julian was getting to know the strange little family a lot better than he'd ever expected. Sometimes, it was a lot more information than he ever wanted to know...

Rae remembered a specific occasion just a few weeks back, when Julian had showed up one evening—looking very concerned.

"Gabriel... He named Angel."

Devon spat out a mouthful of whiskey, while Rae shot forward on the couch.

"What?"

"Yeah." Julian stared into the fire, looking deeply disturbed. "Apparently, she didn't have one when she got there, and Cromfield didn't care what they called her, so he told Gabriel to give her a name."

"And he picked 'Angel'?" Devon was trying very hard to be supportive, but the irony was too much to bear.

Julian flipped him off with a grin, gazing thoughtfully into the fire. "He said he based it off a character in a children's book—the only book he had down in the cave. Said she looked like the angel on the cover."

The flames flickered in his dark eyes as he watched them with a thoughtful frown. Trying to imagine what life must have been like in the darker places in the world.

"They said these things so casually," he murmured, shaking his head with a frown. It was a far cry from the way he looked now. Lit up from the inside out as he counted down the days until he could meet his own child. All golden smiles in the setting sun. "It's...interesting," he said with an evasive grin. "There's something new every day."

Rae chuckled as they stared out at the kids. "Yeah, I'll bet."

She knew firsthand what it was like to try to balance their supernatural lives with a normal pregnancy. The day she'd found out she was pregnant, just a few weeks after their big showdown at the factory, she thought she was going to have a heart attack right there on the living room floor.

Things were looking the same for Julian and Angel. But Rae and Devon were more than willing to help. In fact, one could say they were slightly over-enthusiastic at the news that their best friend was expecting a child. They had even taken to tagging along to them monthly ultrasounds.

Those were also...interesting.

"Now, this is going to be a little cold, but I'm just going to rub it all over your stomach, okay? It's going to help us see that bouncing little bundle of joy!"

Julian and Angel froze in unison, staring warily at the strange woman wielding what looked to be a bottle of lube. Angel's eyes narrowed, and Julian cleared his throat nervously.

"Where's, uh...where's our normal doctor?"

"Oh, she's out at lunch!" the woman replied, bouncing foot to foot as her springy hair danced around her. "I'll be helping you today. It's only my second shift, so I'm a little nervous!"

Julian lifted his eyebrows, while the others glanced contemplatively at the door. It looked like they were actually considering making a break for it, when she reached out and grabbed his arm.

"What an interesting tattoo!" she cried, as cartoonishly chipper as she was wildly oblivious to other people's personal boundaries. "And you!" She spotted Devon at the same time, doubling her delight. "You have one in the same spot! Did you get them at the same time?"

Julian cautiously reclaimed his arm, while Devon shifted nervously on the spot. "Um...kind of, I guess."

Only Rae seemed to find the entire experience greatly amusing. She clapped a hand over her mouth, but not in time to hide the small explosion of giggles that followed.

"They certainly *did* get them at the same time—these two do everything together. Going to the dentist, combing each other's hair. Matching tattoos are just the tip of the iceberg..."

The boys shot her an identical scathing glare, and Angel gestured angrily to her stomach.

"Can we make this a little more about me?" she demanded.

"All right, that's enough!" The door opened just in the nick of time, and Alicia breezed into the room. She took one look at the scene in front of her before dismissing the bubbly technician with a brisk smile. "Kerri, thanks for your help. I can take it from here."

As Kerri waved enthusiastically and skipped outside, Devon turned to Alicia with a low undertone. "Aly, that woman should not be working in medicine."

Julian shuddered in agreement, wiping his arm distractedly against his shirt. "She should be in a banana costume, selling ice cream on the pier."

"Enough, already." Alicia shook her head with an exasperated grin, locking the door behind her. "It's bad enough you guys always have to come on my lunch."

Instead of bothering with the blinking machine in the corner, she ran her hand gently over Angel's stomach. Trancing in and out for a moment, she looked up with a warm smile.

"Congratulations! You have a healthy baby girl. I couldn't even see its little horns…"

Rae returned to the present with a grin, just in time to see her dinner go up in flames.

"Jules?" Devon called suddenly. The world's greatest warrior was staring down at the grill with a rather defeated expression. "I'm in over my head here…"

As Julian went over to help, the children squealed again as someone new came into the yard.

"Uncle Gabriel!"

Rae glanced up in surprise as Molly rolled her eyes with a grin.

"What a shocker. He's late."

As Gabriel greeted the children, Rae abandoned the children and headed quickly across the yard. It wasn't often they saw him these days, and not a moment was to be wasted.

"Hi," she said breathlessly, letting out a little shriek as he scooped her up in the air. "I'm so happy you're here; we weren't expecting to see you!"

His arms wrapped tight around her waist, sneaking ever lower as he clutched her against him, eyes lit up with a mischievous grin. Before Rae had the chance to say anything else, Devon called out routinely from across the yard, his eyes still locked on the smoking grill.

"Gabriel, get your hands off my wife." The children glanced up curiously, and he added a cursory, "please."

Gabriel released her with a grin. "You know, I think he's finally starting to come around to the idea."

Rae shook her head with a smile as the two of them stared out across the yard. By now, the kids had stopped being friends and had decided to destroy each other instead. Benjamin was accomplishing this by shooting pretend sparks out of his hands—accompanied by a series of sound effects—while Aria ran in circles, pelting him with sticks.

A faint grin lit Gabriel's face as he watched them play.

"Our kid would have been cuter, you know."

Impossible. Aria was perfection and they both knew it.

"Doesn't matter who I have a kid with," Rae answered flippantly, tossing back her long raven hair. "The thing's going to look exactly me."

"And thank bloody goodness for that," Gabriel teased.

The two of them laughed quietly before it faded into silence. A minute or two later, Rae glanced at him out of the corner of her eye.

"You're leaving again, aren't you?"

Gabriel didn't answer. He simply stared across the lawn.

Rae's chest tightened with a sigh. "I wish I could come with you."

He looked down with a gentle smile. "No, you don't. You've fought hard for this, Rae." His eyes flickered across the lawn, coming to rest on her little girl. "You can't walk away now."

"Then why won't you stay?" she reasoned quietly. "And don't give me your usual bullsh-crap answer. You know that doesn't work on me."

He chuckled quickly, still staring out at the lawn. "You never know." When she sighed again he turned to her at once, tilting up her chin with that same sparkling smile. "I meant, you never know what might happen."

Her eyes lit up hopefully and he gave her a wink.

"I can think of one or two reasons to stick around..."

"Dinner's ready!"

Without another word, they joined the others at the table. The adults helped settle the children, while the older generation sat back with a knowing smile. They were right about to start passing around the plates, when the door burst open and Carter rushed into the yard.

"I know, I know. I'm late! I'm sorry!"

Aria let out a squeal of joy when she saw him, leaping quickly out of Devon's arms and racing across the yard. Carter scooped her up without a moment's pause. The stress and tension vanished from his face the second she was in his arms. "How was your day, sunshine?"

Her face brightened impossibly as a tumble of raven curls danced across her cheeks.

"I ate a bug!" she declared proudly.

Rae and Devon looked up with a start as Carter passed her off to Beth, sinking with an amused chuckle into his chair. "And *that*...is the perfect end to a horrible day."

"That's what you get for being president," Rae chided teasingly. "Horrible days."

He poured himself a drink, and leaned back in his chair. "Would you like to try it?"

"Are you kidding?" She shuddered at the very thought. "Not for anything in the world."

His eyes sharpened slightly as they fell upon Devon at the far end of the table. "Of course, my day would have gone a lot better if your husband had finished his mission report on time."

Devon set down his beer with a look of supplication. "I had to get back for Aria's dance recital. I said I'd finish it in the morning."

Carter rubbed his eyes with a long-suffering sigh. "A dance recital. My top agent comes to me with a dance recital. The world we live in..."

"Sir, it really wasn't his fault," Julian intervened gently, coming automatically to his best friend's defense. "I can help him finish it up in the morning."

Carter glanced up, his eyes flickering down to the daisy on Julian's face. "I rest my case."

"Enough work talk," Beth demanded, raising her glass with a twinkling smile. "We came here today for a reason. Three years ago, my beautiful daughter married the world's most wonderful man. Congratulations, sweetie. It looks like you finally got that future you always wanted."

Three years. Has it really been three years?

Rae remembered it like it was only yesterday...

The ceremony had been small. Intimate. A far cry from the extravagant royal wedding they'd attended just a few months before. They had gone back to the cliffs of Scotland. To the very same place, in fact, where Devon had gotten down on his knee at sunset and proposed.

He had been so *nervous*.

A nostalgic smile flashed across Rae's face as she remembered. Even with a gun pointed to his head, Rae had never seen him so scared. He fidgeted and twitched nervously in his suit until, finally, Angel offered to give him a dose of her blood to steady the nerves. He politely declined.

"Okay, are you ready?" Molly had said, smoothing down the back of Rae's dress as her mother handed off the bouquet. "I can tell Carter to hold off if you want to take a minute."

They had gotten the dress together in a boutique just a few weeks before. The same boutique where Molly returned a few days later to purchase a dress of her own.

"No, I'm ready." Rae took a deep breath as she stared outside the conjured tent at the beautifully breathtaking ocean view. "More than ready."

"It's a good thing, too," Beth teased gently. "Andrew has been practicing the ceremony day and night. He'll have a coronary if you make him wait."

Both women kissed her gently on the cheek before walking down the grass aisle. They had kept things simple. No ornamentation. No frills. Just the people they loved most in the world gathered together on the rocky cliffs. Their beloved family, standing by their side.

Rae wanted until they reached the end before stepping slowly from the tent. The warm summer breeze swept her hair around her as she stared towards the horizon, and into Devon's eyes.

He was enchanting. Her own fairytale prince come to life.

Standing tall against the brilliant sunset, his entire face was haloed in a golden glow. From his dark hair, to his breathtaking smile, to his sparkling eyes—eyes that stared back at Rae as if he was lost in a dream.

The music started, and with a little smile she started walking towards him...

"To the future!"

Rae snapped back to the present as the others echoed the chant. Her eyes flickered automatically to her husband before coming to rest on his ring. It was a ring she had conjured herself. Made with all the best parts of her. Made with the deepest kind of love.

"To the future."

Their eyes met and they shared a radiant smile.

Because we finally have one. A future to call our own.

A silent tear slipped down her face as she turned to the psychic sitting by her side. "What do you think, Jules? Is it going to be a good one?"

He laughed quickly, shaking his head with a little grin. "Well, of course I can't tell you that. But I *can* tell you this..." His eyes twinkled as he and the rest of the friends gazed into the horizon.

"Wait!" Rae grinned. "Let me tell them." She inhaled, taking in the view. "It's going to be worth the wait."

THE END (but turn the page)

GABRIEL – BOOK 1 BLURB

How can you build a future, when a part of you is trapped in the past?

Gabriel Alden's problems were supposed to be over. The man who had enslaved him had been destroyed. The girl he was supposed to kill had become his saving grace. And the people he had been sent to infiltrate had ended up as family. So why, when everyone else had found their happily-ever-after, was Gabriel still out in the cold?

Dark memories, hidden shadows, and secrets too terrible to imagine haunt his every breath—chasing after him as he races around the globe, searching for the truth.

Can he ever truly escape his past? Will he ever have a shot at a future? How far can you run before your ghosts finally catch up with you?

One thing is certain: Gabriel's problems are just getting started...

** Chapter Excerpt **

Chapter 1

Gabriel Alden stared silently up at the ceiling, watching as the golden sunset cast long shadows along the wall. It was getting late. Around six or seven in the evening, but one of the good things about never having a place to be was that you were never in a hurry. His bright eyes locked onto the progression of the sun, following in a slow arc as it leisurely made its way across the room.

The air was thick and warm, scented with the intoxicating fragrance of the thousand climbing flowers that lined the streets of Prague. He breathed in deeply, closing his eyes for a moment as it washed over him.

I was right to come here. This is the place. I can feel it.

An angry vibration on the table shattered his peaceful meditation—yanking him back to the present with a gasp of surprise. He cast a quick glance at the naked woman sleeping beside him before reaching towards it—the damp sheets twisting around his waist as he grabbed it off the bedside table.

One look at the screen, and his shoulders fell with a tired sigh. Rae Kerrigan had texted him every week since he'd left. Each one was more anxious than the last.

Gabriel, where the hell are you? The least you could do is call.

Seriously. We're getting really worried.

Okay, fine. ME. I'm getting worried.

Alright, Alden—enough is enough. If you won't write back to me, then at least write back to your sister. She's driving everyone over here crazy worrying about you.

Devon says you probably fell off a boat and got eaten by alligators somewhere in the Amazon. He doesn't seem too broken up about it.

Gabriel actually had to smile at that last one. No, he didn't think Devon would be too broken up about it. Not considering how long Gabriel had been after his girl.

A faint smile flashed across his face as his fingers hovered over the keys. Wondering what to write back. But a second later, he set the phone back down on the table.

What would he say? The best he could hope to do was a lie—and he didn't like to do that.

Not to Rae.

There was a soft rustling of fabric beside him, and he quickly lay back down. Watching as the bewitching woman beside him slowly opened her eyes.

"Good morning," he said softly. "You slept a long time."

With good reason. Their antics the night before had continued into the early hours of the morning. And then a little longer after that.

She gazed up at him with a sleepy smile before deliberately tossing the sheets off her naked body—letting him feast his eyes. He chuckled appreciatively, then trailed a finger down the line of her stomach. Her skin was smooth. Warm. Wanting.

"You did not sleep?"

The hand disappeared. So did the smile that had come with it.

"No," he said shortly, rolling onto his back. "No sleep."

The sheets rustled again as she climbed onto his chest, tracing the tip of her finger along his lips before stretching up to give him a kiss. He did so robotically. Routinely. His mind was a million miles away. But his lips still twitched up into the obligatory grin when she pulled away.

"You make me breakfast?"

A short laugh burst out of him, warming his eyes with a genuine smile. His arms wrapped around her back, holding her tight to his skin.

"Demanding little thing, aren't you?" She shrugged coyly, and he laughed again. "I like you far too much to subject you to my cooking."

What was her name again? Eva? Ava? It was something short.

She nodded slowly, bowing her head to kiss his tan skin, gazing back up with a tentative smile. "Then, maybe...we do other things?"

Gabriel exhaled slowly, gazing at her in the golden light. He was neither particularly excited nor particularly inclined—but she was kind, and sweet, and warm. Just like the last girl had been. And the girl before that. And the girl before that.

To be honest, he had woken up in so many beds these last few months he was having trouble keeping track...

"You ever been to England?" he asked, feeling suddenly homesick.

He spoke in quiet English, grateful that she could understand. His Czech wasn't what it used to be. She glanced up at him, then shook her head—returning her lips to his skin.

"It's beautiful," he continued softly, staring up at the ceiling as she wrapped her legs around his waist—pulling herself up to straddle him. "Colder than here. But beautiful."

Her hair spilled down her shoulders as she trailed her fingers up his chest.

"London is crazy this time of year." A sudden smile flashed across his face as he remembered. "I actually have some friends who are—"

"You want to go to London?" she interrupted sharply. "Or you want to be here with me?"

He fell instantly silent, staring up at her in surprise, a little grin creeping up the side of her face. In a flash, he flipped them both over. Landing on top of her, he pinned her arms firmly above her head.

"Like I said, you're a demanding little thing..."

He lowered his lips to hers, but a second before they could touch a deafening bang shook the door in its frame. They pulled apart at once, staring with wide eyes. For a split second, all was quiet. Then the door rattled again—sending little bits of plaster shaking off the frame.

Gabriel sprang to his feet, searching desperately for his pants as twenty years of predatory instincts kicked into place. The shirt was forgotten, but there was a knife in the inner pocket of his coat. A second later, it was in his hands as he waited in the center of the room.

"Stay there," he murmured, eyes dilating as they locked on the handle. "Just stay where you are—cover your eyes."

"What?!"

The blankets flew off in a mad scramble as the woman without a name leapt to her feet and raced to the floor in front of him—steadying his hand.

"What are you doing?!" she demanded in a panicked hiss. "That is my husband. You aim to kill him?"

The knife lowered an inch.

"Your...husband?"

Her eyes widened desperately as she stared at the blade. She was only slightly more comforted when he slipped it back into his pocket. "Yes—my husband. I told you last night I was married. Zenaty—married."

Gabriel's handsome face blanked.

"I thought zenaty meant: I'm single and my place is just at the end of the block."

I've got to brush up on this damn language.

"No!" she shrieked as the door shook again. One more hard knock, and it was coming down. "You've got to get out of here!

Quick!" A blast of warm air hit his face as she opened the window—cocking her head towards the three-story drop below.

For a second, all he did was stare. Then the door shuddered again, and a slow smile crept up the side of his face. A husband. Given the sorts of problems he was used to dealing with, a disgruntled husband was relatively normal.

"Well, my love, it seems I've overstayed my welcome." He gave her a roguish kiss before leaping up into the window. "My best regards to your husband."

He leapt into the air just as the door banged open. Just in time to see the reddened face of what had to be the biggest, angriest man he'd ever seen. He landed with a thud on a fire escape two floors below, then leapt the rest of the way down.

The second he landed on the cobblestone the man appeared above him. Leaning over the balcony and screaming a litany of oaths so dark, an old woman in an apartment across the street closed the shutters. Gabriel squinted up at him, shielding his eyes against the setting sun.

"That word, I did know..."

A ceramic flower pot shattered on the wall above his head, and he took off sprinting down the street. Wishing he'd taken that extra second to find his shoes.

Please, let the psychic not be seeing his. Julian, keep your eyes to yourself.

He didn't stop running until he'd reached the main city square. By the time he did, the sun had already slipped below the horizon. He slowed to a gradual stop, glancing warily around him, putting his hands on his knees to catch his breath. A pair of women walking past giggled and waved, and he abruptly remembered that in addition to having lost his shoes he had also forgotten his shirt.

"Fucking fantastic."

He glanced around again, looking for a store that might still be open, when a sudden vibration buzzed the pocket of his jeans. A ringtone was soon to follow. "God Bless the Queen."

His eyes closed in a pained grimace before he reached down to answer. No way to put it off any longer. And no reason to glance at the screen. He already knew who was calling.

"Rae, now's not really the best time."

There was a slight pause. Followed by an explosion.

"Gabriel!" She was shocked, angry, and delighted—all at the same time. "I can't believe you actually picked up! I was getting ready to leave you another message!"

"Well, we can always try that instead—"

"Gabriel—where the hell are you? When are you coming home?"

He stifled a sigh. Hearing her voice hurt more than he thought it would.

And home was kind of a relative term at the moment.

"You know, Kerrigan, the point of these existential expeditions is to get some time by yourself. To clear your head, and try to find a new perspective. Alone. Undisturbed." He paused, glancing sideways at the phone. "Did I mention *alone*?"

Was that part getting through to her? Probably not.

"When are you coming home?" she said again. The same words that Angel hounded him with every day. "Things are—and I miss—tried to tell you—"

"Rae?" He glanced down at the phone, then held it back to his ear. "Rae, the line's breaking up."

There was crackling pause.

"Gabriel, the line's breaking up."

He rubbed his eyes wearily, trying to stave off the beginnings of a hangover.

"Yeah, gorgeous—I kind of want it to."

"What was that?" Her voice sounded a world away. Much farther than just the hundreds of miles he'd put between them. "Gabriel, I can't hear you, so just promise me you're okay."

"Yeah, I'm okay—"

"Just say that you're okay, otherwise I'm coming to get you."

"Rae, for the last time. I swear to you, I'm—"

The line went dead.

"—fine."

He slowly pulled the phone away from his face, and stared down at the darkened screen. His frantic pacing had taken him away from the main roads of the city. To a little side street that overlooked the bustle and noise, without really being a part of it.

"I'm fine," he said again, standing in the center of the deserted street. No one was there to hear him. Everyone he cared about in the entire world was miles away. "...fine."

The sounds of raucous laughter filtered into the alley, punctuated with the cloying smell of alcohol. He gazed for a moment in its general direction before the combination pulled him forward towards yet another bar. The streetlamps came on, and silver moonlight danced bright upon the wet cobblestones as he walked back out onto the street.

Prague did two things well. Bars and women. The rest didn't matter, because you'd never remember it when you woke up.

This was one of those dive bars. The kind the good people of the Czech Republic kept purposely off the maps to keep tourists from wandering inside. He stared up at the flickering neon light for a moment, listening to the mayhem raging on behind the walls before his shoulders fell with a little sigh.

Then the door pushed open, and he slipped inside without another word. Vanishing into the darkness. Hoping to soon find himself at the bottom of a bottle.

Chasing after that ever-elusive 'fine.'

COMING JULY 15th

PREORDER YOUR COPY TODAY!

The Chronicles of Kerrigan

Book I - *Rae of Hope* is FREE!
  Book Trailer:
  http://www.youtube.com/watch?v=gILAwXxx8MU
  Book II - *Dark Nebula*
  Book Trailer:
  http://www.youtube.com/watch?v=Ca24STi_bFM
  Book III - *House of Cards*
  Book IV - *Royal Tea*
  Book V - *Under Fire*
  Book VI - *End in Sight*
  Book VII – *Hidden Darkness*
  Book VIII – *Twisted Together*
  Book IX – *Mark of Fate*
  Book X – *Strength & Power*
  Book XI – *Last One Standing*
  BOOK XII – *Rae of Light*

PREQUEL –
  Christmas Before the Magic
  Question the Darkness

Into the Darkness
Fight the Darkness
Alone the Darkness
Lost the Darkness

SEQUEL –
    Matter of Time
    Time Piece
    Second Chance
    Glitch in Time
    Our Time
    Precious Time

More books by W.J. May

Hidden Secrets Saga:
Download Seventh Mark part 1 For FREE
Book Trailer:
http://www.youtube.com/watch?v=Y-_vVYC1gvo

Like most teenagers, Rouge is trying to figure out who she is and what she wants to be. With little knowledge about her past, she has questions but has never tried to find the answers. Everything changes when she befriends a strangely intoxicating family. Siblings Grace and Michael, appear to have secrets which seem connected to Rouge. Her hunch is confirmed when a horrible incident occurs at an outdoor party. Rouge may be the only one who can find the answer.

An ancient journal, a Sioghra necklace and a special mark force life-altering decisions for a girl who grew up unprepared to fight for her life or others.

All secrets have a cost and Rouge's determination to find the truth can only lead to trouble...or something even more sinister.

RADIUM HALOS - THE SENSELESS SERIES
Book 1 is FREE

Everyone needs to be a hero at one point in their life. The small town of Elliot Lake will never be the same again. Caught in a sudden thunderstorm, Zoe, a high school senior from Elliot Lake, and five of her friends take shelter in an abandoned uranium mine. Over the next few days, Zoe's hearing sharpens drastically, beyond what any normal human being can detect. She tells her friends, only to learn that four others have an increased sense as well. Only Kieran, the new boy from Scotland, isn't affected.

Fashioning themselves into superheroes, the group tries to stop the strange occurrences happening in their little town. Muggings, break-ins, disappearances, and murder begin to hit too close to home. It leads the team to think someone knows about their secret - someone who wants them all dead.

An incredulous group of heroes. A traitor in the midst. Some dreams are written in blood.

Courage Runs Red
The Blood Red Series
Book 1 is FREE

What if courage was your only option?

When Kallie lands a college interview with the city's new hot-shot police officer, she has no idea everything in her life is about to change. The detective is young, handsome and seems to have an unnatural ability to stop the increasing local crime rate. Detective Liam's particular interest in Kallie sends her heart and head stumbling over each other.

When a raging blood feud between vampires spills into her home, Kallie gets caught in the middle. Torn between love and family loyalty she must find the courage to fight what she fears the most and possibly risk everything, even if it means dying for those she loves.

Daughter of Darkness
<u>Victoria</u>
Only Death Could Stop Her Now
The Daughters of Darkness is a series of female heroines who may or may not know each other, but all have the same father, Vlad Montour.
Victoria is a Hunter Vampire

Coming Soon:

TUDOR COMPARISON:

Aumbry House—A recess to hold sacred vessels, often found in castle chapels.
  Aumbry House was considered very special to hold the female students - their sacred vessels (especially Rae Kerrigan).

Joist House—A timber stretched from wall-to-wall to support floorboards.
  Joist House was considered a building of support where the male students could support and help each other.

Oratory—A private chapel in a house.
  Private education room in the school where the students were able to practice their gifting and improve their skills. Also used as a banquet - dance hall when needed.

Oriel—A projecting window in a wall; originally a form of porch, often of wood. The original bay windows of the Tudor period. Guilder College majority of windows were oriel.
  Rae often felt her life was being watching through one of these windows. Hence the constant reference to them.

Refectory—A communal dining hall. Same termed used in Tudor times.

Scriptorium—A Medieval writing room in which scrolls were also housed.
  Used for English classes and still store some of the older books from the Tudor reign (regarding tatùs).

Privy Council—Secret council and "arm of the government" similar to the CIA, etc... In Tudor times, the Privy Council was King Henry's board of advisors and helped run the country.

Don't miss out!

Click the button below and you can sign up to receive emails whenever W.J. May publishes a new book. There's no charge and no obligation.

[Sign Me Up!]

https://books2read.com/r/B-A-SSF-XJGN

BOOKS 2 READ

Connecting independent readers to independent writers.

Did you love *Precious Time*? Then you should read *Living in the Past* by W.J. May!

The past is your lesson. The present is your gift. The future is your motivation.

From USA Today bestselling author, W.J. May brings you a spin off from the Chronicles of Kerrigan. This is a stand alone series, or can be read with the Chronicles of Kerrigan series

How can you build a future, when a part of you is trapped in the past?

Gabriel Alden's problems were supposed to be over. The man who had enslaved him had been destroyed. The girl he was supposed to kill, had become his saving grace. And the people he had been sent to infiltrate, had ended up as family. So why, when everyone else had found their happy-ever-after, was Gabriel still out in the cold?

Dark memories, hidden shadows, and secrets too terrible to imagine haunt his every breath—chasing after him as he races around the globe, searching for the truth.

Can he ever truly escape his past? Will he ever have a shot at a future? How far can you run before your ghosts finally catch up with you?

One thing is certain, Gabriel's problems are just getting started...

The Chronicles of Kerrigan: Gabriel
Living in the Past
Present for Today
Staring at the Future

READ THE WHOLE SERIES:

Prequel Series:
Christmas Before the Magic
Question the Darkness
Into the Darkness
Fight the Darkness
Alone in the Darkness
Lost in Darkness

The Chronicles of Kerrigan Series
Rae of Hope
Dark Nebula
House of Cards
Royal Tea
Under Fire
End in Sight
Hidden Darkness
Twisted Together
Mark of Fate
Strength & Power

Last	One			Standing
Rae of Light				
The	Chronicles	of	Kerrigan	Sequel
A	Matter		of	Time
Time				Piece
Second				Chance
Glitch		in		Time
Our				Time
Precious Time				

Also by W.J. May

Bit-Lit Series
Lost Vampire
Cost of Blood
Price of Death

Blood Red Series
Courage Runs Red
The Night Watch
Marked by Courage
Forever Night

Daughters of Darkness: Victoria's Journey
Victoria
Huntress
Coveted (A Vampire & Paranormal Romance)
Twisted

Hidden Secrets Saga
Seventh Mark - Part 1
Seventh Mark - Part 2
Marked By Destiny
Compelled
Fate's Intervention
Chosen Three
The Hidden Secrets Saga: The Complete Series

Prophecy Series
Only the Beginning

The Chronicles of Kerrigan

Rae of Hope
Dark Nebula
House of Cards
Royal Tea
Under Fire
End in Sight
Hidden Darkness
Twisted Together
Mark of Fate
Strength & Power
Last One Standing
Rae of Light
The Chronicles of Kerrigan Box Set Books # 1 - 6

The Chronicles of Kerrigan: Gabriel
Living in the Past

The Chronicles of Kerrigan Prequel
Christmas Before the Magic
Question the Darkness
Into the Darkness
Fight the Darkness
Alone in the Darkness
Lost in Darkness
The Chronicles of Kerrigan Prequel Series Books #1-3

The Chronicles of Kerrigan Sequel
A Matter of Time
Time Piece
Second Chance
Glitch in Time
Our Time
Precious Time

The Hidden Secrets Saga
Seventh Mark (part 1 & 2)

The Senseless Series
Radium Halos
Radium Halos - Part 2
Nonsense

Standalone
Shadow of Doubt (Part 1 & 2)
Five Shades of Fantasy
Shadow of Doubt - Part 2
Four and a Half Shades of Fantasy
Full Moon
Dream Fighter
What Creeps in the Night
Forest of the Forbidden
HuNted
Arcane Forest: A Fantasy Anthology
Ancient Blood of the Vampire and Werewolf

Made in the USA
Middletown, DE
03 May 2018